If You Cross Me Once 2

Anthony Fields

If You Cross Me Once 2

Lock Down Publications and Ca$h Presents
If You Cross Me Once 2
A Novel by *Anthony Fields*

Anthony Fields

Lock Down Publications
P.O. Box 944
Stockbridge, Ga 30281

Visit our website @
www.lockdownpublications.com

Copyright 2022 Anthony Fields
If You Cross Me Once 2

All rights reserved. No part of this book may be reproduced in any form or by electronic or mechanical means, including information storage and retrieval systems without permission in writing from the publisher, except by a reviewer who may quote brief passages in review.
First Edition December 2022
Printed in the United States of America

This is a work of fiction. Names, characters, places, and incidents either are products of the author's imagination or are used fictitiously. Any similarity to actual events or locales or persons, living or dead, is entirely coincidental.

Lock Down Publications
Like our page on Facebook: **Lock Down Publications** @
www.facebook.com/lockdownpublications.ldp
Cover design and layout by: **Dynasty Cover Me**
Book interior design by: **Shawn Walker**

If You Cross Me Once 2

Stay Connected with Us!

Text **LOCKDOWN** to 22828 to stay up-to-date with new releases, sneak peaks, contests and more…
Thank you.

Anthony Fields

Submission Guideline.

Submit the first three chapters of your completed manuscript to ldpsubmissions@gmail.com, subject line: Your book's title. The manuscript must be in a .doc file and sent as an attachment. Document should be in Times New Roman, double spaced and in size 12 font. Also, provide your synopsis and full contact information. If sending multiple submissions, they must each be in a separate email.

Have a story but no way to send it electronically? You can still submit to LDP/Ca$h Presents. Send in the first three chapters, written or typed, of your completed manuscript to:

LDP: Submissions Dept
P.O. Box 944
Stockbridge, Ga 30281

DO NOT send original manuscript. Must be a duplicate.

Provide your synopsis and a cover letter containing your full contact information.

Thanks for considering LDP and Ca$h Presents.

If You Cross Me Once 2

THIS BOOK IS DEDICATED TO ALL THE GOOD MEN WHO'VE BEEN TOLD ON BY A RAT BASTARD.

Anthony Fields

Acknowledgements

I often write these acknowledgements and vent about anything that's on my mind at that time. It's like writing in a diary. I've had dudes write me and tell me that they were feeling my acknowledgements the most. I don't know whether to be happy about that or sad. As these days fly by and I continue to grow and learn, I understand life better. Life is a constant progression that doesn't stop until you're dead. I remember things that were said to me ten, twenty, and even thirty years ago and realize that a lot of what was predicted has actually come to pass. It's like I looked into a crystal ball, but instead of seeing the future, I see the past. Someone told me before that if you don't learn from your past, you'll repeat it and make it your future. Back then, they were just empty words to me. Today they are profound.

I sit in this federal penitentiary, a place I entered in 1994, a place from my past that I've made into my future, all because I didn't learn from my past mistakes. It's 2022. I literally grew up in these federal pens. USP's, not FCI's. Trust me, there's a difference. Correction: there used to be a difference. I have been all across this country in prison and I can't believe how bad things are now. I can't believe how much the principle fabric of these joints have eroded to nothing. I can't believe the overt acceptance of all things perverted and creepish. Because I choose not to pull my penis out and jack off of female staff, I'm considered weird. The inmates with immoral and unbalanced characters are the exalted ones, while the cold-blooded men are ostracized, slept on, and slandered. Just as time diminishes the muscle and getting old becomes a reality, it's always hard to accept that your body can no longer do what your mind thinks it can. So is the understanding that the old guard has to give way to the new. Old warriors and soldiers get replaced with newer, younger ones. Old morals and principles become replaced with new ones. Just as the old testament in the bible had to give way to the new testament, the old law becomes the new law, no matter how messed up it may be. I'm an older convict trying to explain old values, morals, and principles to millennial minds, and it ain't working. I digress. To all the people that I love, you know who you are. To all the people that I don't mess with, you know who you are. All praise is due to Allah. To my son, Kevin, and my daughter, Aniyah, I hope to leave behind a legacy that y'all can be proud of.

I wasn't going to do a lot of name dropping in this one but I'm being pressured to shout out a few good men. To all the good men in Hazelton with me: Mike "88" David, Larry Wilkerson, Nykemia "Bey" Everette, Fat Sean aka Birdman, K Boogie, Tye, Chunky, Peter Paul, Ray, Curt, Remedan, Lawrence "El" Wilkerson, Marquette, "D-Man" Tibbs, Keon, Poo Poo, John "Buck" Rayner, Mike, B-More Mel, Who Dat, Fish Sub, Old head Player, Gay-Bey, Marco, CJ, Antonio, Tay Bullock, Dave, Block, None, Cliff, Vee, Floyd-El, Fred, E, Big Wali, Tweez, Clip, Jo Jo, An, Rock, Rick, Small-Bey, Blessing, BX Que, LD, Florida Bruce, Bunz, Shipre, Wax (Florida), Rell, Sneeze, Flavor, Lamont, Sleepy, Smizz, Silk (Louisville, Kentucky), Bobby, Wayne Wayne (Capers), and others.

To Face, Boosie, Nightlife, Hitman, Nut (Yonkers), Duke (Newark) Gotti, Price, Styles (Plainfield), Pyrex, San, Certified, Strong, Ghost (640), Teddy (B-more) Antbone, Nitty, Von, Slut, Flash (Portsmouth, VA),/Chuck, Supreme, CB, Suave, Moe, Steelz, Bert, Flint, Lil G, Drew, Ice, Rose, Bro Muhammad, Turk, Rude Bouoi, Knight, JR, Brooklyn Rell, Miami Rob and several more that I can't remember.

Shout out to Jamel Mitchell, the author of FOR THE LOVE OF BLOOD, and to all the good men who made it home this year.

You already know what it is.

D.C., stand up!

Buckeyfields

Anthony Fields

If You Cross Me Once 2

Chapter 1
QURAN

"Hey, baby. I'm in a coffee shop on M Street, about to order a large cup of Brazilian hazelnut coffee," Zin said.

"That's what's up. I'ma handle some business with a friend and then call you later," I replied.

"Make sure you do. I got good news from my father's lawyer. I'm just leaving his office in Georgetown. I'm thinking about going to the condo and getting the rest of my things from there."

"Do you need me to pull up?"

"Naw, I'm good. Jermaine ain't crazy. If he's there, I'll just grab a few things and go. Probably won't even talk to his ass. You go ahead and do you. I'll call you if I need you."

"A'ight, bet. I'ma hit you later on. Love you, Zin."

"Love you too. Bye."

The call ended. I dropped my phone into my lap and looked over at Sean. His eyes were closed as he leaned back in his seat.

"Do you think it's a good idea to be fucking with shorty like that?"

I thought about the question that Sean had just asked before replying. "Sometimes I think it is and sometimes I think it ain't. I never meant to fall in love with Zin. I really just wanted to fuck her. But then my feelings got involved because she made me chase her."

"You never stopped to think about who she was, your connection to her family, and the obvious conflict of interest?"

"Not at first, no. But by the time it really hit me, I was already in too deep."

"Does she know anything about what you do for her father? What you've always done for him?"

"Naw. She don't know shit. And that's the way I plan to keep it."

"That's a recipe for disaster, Que. You know it and I know it. Too many secrets, young'un. Does Mike know that you fucking with his daughter?"

"Fuck no," I stated emphatically. "He wouldn't approve."

11

"So, if you know that, why would you still do it?" Sean asked.

"I don't know. Like I said, originally, I was just tryna fuck because she looked good as shit. Never even thought about the fact that she was Mike's daughter."

"But now?"

"Now, I really love her, big homie. The rest I gotta figure out later."

"Good luck on that, young'un."

Sean got quiet and the silence in the vehicle grew loud. Then a vibrating sound screamed out. I grabbed my phone, but saw that it wasn't my phone. It was Sean's.

"As salaam alaikum," Sean said into the phone as he answered it. "That's a bet, Ock. Hold him right there. I'll be there as soon as I finish up doing what I'm doing. What? Fuck I care about that? Do what the fuck I just said and sit tight with that nigga." Sean put his phone on the middle console. He never opened his eyes once. "When we leave here, we got one more stop to make."

"Say less." I sat back and stared out the window from the passenger seat. The caravan was parked across from a high-rise condominium building. The neighborhood was near the Woodley Park Zoo. It was upper class, affluent, and inhabited by mostly whites. "You sure Kenny Sparrow lives in that building?"

Sean nodded, then went back to wherever his thoughts were.

"He gotta be one of the only black muthafuckas that live around here."

"Probably is. A rat that lives near a zoo. Go figure."

I took in the scene that surrounded 3321 Connecticut Avenue. There was a Neiman Marcus and a Saks Fifth Avenue up the street. There was a Nordstrom Rack and a Maggiano's on the next block. "You gotta be caked up to live around here."

"Kenny been stealing money since the eighties and he ain't never been to jail, so it don't surprise me that he got enough money to live in a neighborhood like this. Kenny is connected to cops and prosecutors. He probably got a witness voucher like a Section Eight joint. The witness protection program might've put him up around here. Do you still smell them bodies that was in here?"

"Hell yeah, I smell that shit. Shit stinks like shit. You sittin' over there acting like you don't smell that shit."

"I gotta get this joint detailed before I take it back. I thought you had your shoes off."

I laughed at that. "Shit, nigga, if anything, that's your breath smelling like that."

Sean cracked up laughing, but he never opened his eyes.

"On a serious note, what's the plan? How we gon' get in there to Kenny?"

"Just fall back, young'un. You gon' see in a minute."

Taking Sean's advice, I fell back. I leaned my seat back and closed my eyes, too. It didn't take long for Zin to pop into my head. No matter where I was or what I was doing, Zin was never far from my thoughts. My cell phone vibrated. I picked up the phone and saw that the caller was Kiki Swinson. "Kiki, what's up?"

"Hey, Que. ain't nothing up. I was just missing your sexy ass. Were you busy?"

"Kinda sorta. But I can talk. What's up?"

"You keep asking me what's up. Ain't nothing up, nigga. I just miss you. Is something wrong with that?"

"Naw. That's what's up. And I miss you, too."

"So when will I get to see you again?" Kiki asked.

"You tell me. You're the bestselling author, doing tours and all that."

"I'm flying out to L.A. tomorrow," Kiki said. "Got a meeting with some people from Netflix about turning one of my books into a movie. I'ma be gone for about five days. Then I'll be back on the east coast. Either I can pit stop in D.C. or you can come down to Virginia Beach again. It's up to you."

"Right now, it's looking like a pit stop, but in five days, that may change. By the time you ready to fly back this way, I should know for sure what we gon' do. Is that good with you?"

"Of course it is. No worries. Whatever you want, Que."

"I'm glad to hear about the book to movie thing, too. Are you going to be in the movie?"

"Maybe. I might do a cameo appearance."

"I ain't never fucked nobody that been in a movie before."

"Well, if you play your cards right, you gon' get your chance to. Stay tuned," Kiki said seductively.

"What book are they tryna turn into a movie?"

"*Candy Shop*. The one I did with Wahida Clark."

"Wahida Clark? She's the one that put out that *Ultimate Sacrifice* joint for my homie, right?"

"Yup. Damn, you still remember that book, huh? You must've really liked it."

"How could I not? It was in my city. Written by a real nigga and raw. I'm waiting on parts three and four to drop. But anyway, congrats on the movie thing. You gon' kill the meeting. Hit me when you on your way back this way."

"I will. Be safe, baby. Bye," Kiki said and ended the call. I turned to Sean. "When you was doing all that time, did you read any of them urban novel joints?"

"You told me that you fucking with that chick Kiki Swinson. That was her on the phone" Sean asked me.

I nodded my head.

"Wild bitch, there, Que. I never said nothing about it, but I was in the joint with her husband. Good bamma named Julien Seay. They call him Juice. All that nigga talk about is that bitch. She's his claim to fame."

"Husband?" I said and laughed. "Get the fuck outta here! If shorty was married, she would been told me. I ain't never seen her wear no ring. Ever. Maybe they just on some jail married shit She wifey and he 'hubby'. You know how that shit go."

"Now, bruh, they really married. Marriage certificate and the whole shebang. Juice a good nigga, I fucks with him. And the homies fuck with him. He writes books, too. But fuck it, he in the bing and she out in the world doing her. That's how shit go. I just wanted to wise you up on her with your tender dick ass. Captain 'save these hoes' ass, young nigga," Sean teased and laughed.

"I ain't got no tender dick, old head. Watch your mouth."

Sean laughed harder.

"And I ain't saving no hoes. You got me twisted."

"A'ight, grey-eyed lover boy. Whatever you say. But to answer your question, of course I read a rack of them urban novel joints. Who didn't? Them novels were the shit when they came out. Teri Woods, Shannon Holmes, Nikki Turner, Wahida, T. Styles, Sistah Souljah, all them Triple Crown joints. My man Al-Saadiq Banks. Your girl Kiki's joints, the *Wifey* series. I was gone off them joints. Then over time, they got watered down, so I decided to write one."

"You? Fuck outta here, slim. You ain't write no book."

Sean picked up his phone and pulled up something, then passed me the phone.

"I tried to get the bitch Vickie Stringer to put my book out. She owned that Triple Crown joint. But then I found out the bitch was hot. Told on some Jamaicans that was getting money in Columbus, Ohio. She wanted to fuck with me, but I curved her ass. I ain't fuckin' with no rats. I hollered at a bitch named Crystal Perkins in Oklahoma and self-published my shit."

Sure enough, on the screen of the phone was Amazon.com with a book available for purchase titled, *Money, Murder, and Mayhem*, by Sean Branch. "Damn, big homie, you wasn't bullshittin'. How long this joint been out?"

"A few years now. Surprised you didn't know."

"Never heard a word about it. I'ma cop it, though. ASAP. Is it real shit or some made up shit?" I turned to face Sean.

Sean looked at me and gave me the "do I look stupid?" face. "All fiction got a degree of truth to it. But I couldn't do too much because then niggas will say a nigga hot."

"About something you put in an urban novel?" I was confused.

"No doubt. Remember this, Que. Ain't nobody exempt from slander. Nobody."

"Cut that shit out, slim. Your street rep is legendary. That alone would shield you from slander. Niggas already know…"

"Fuck that, young boy Que. Like I said, ain't nobody bigger than the bones that niggas can put on a nigga. Street reps don't shield niggas and lies don't care who tell 'em. They just tryna be told. See, here's the thing, young'un. There's a major disconnect between my era and yours. This new generation is fucked up. They can't think past go. I had to be extra careful what I put in the book because if niggas believe they read something remotely real, they gon' call me hot. In my era, if two niggas kill somebody and get locked up, then one of them dies, it's understood that you put the body on the dead man. Why? Because dead men can't face prosecution. There's no harm that can come to him. He's dead. Makes all the sense in the world, right? But young niggas, niggas in your era, say that's hot. To them, all the old law shit is fucked up. And ain't none of this new shit hot. Getting on Instagram Live and Facebook Live calling out the real names of their ops ain't hot to them. Telling all your followers on the Gram that Ridge Road beefing with Clay Terrace and that they about to 'spin the bend' ain't hot. Going on social media and talking about street beefs, real time murders, and all that ain't hot to young niggas. Talkin' to your ops, pulling out guns, and telling them to 'pull up' ain't hot. Commenting on niggas pages that Jay Jay killed John John ain't hot to them. The feds monitor all that shit and they know that, but still talk reckless on social sites."

"That's some dumb-ass shit, slim. I ain't with none of that shit," I stressed with conviction. "I be going on Jihad n'em about that shit."

"These young niggas hitting licks, then post the pictures with what they got from the lick, still wearing the clothes they hit the lick in. When they get bagged, the first thing they say is that somebody told. Naw, nigga - you told! On you and your men that hit the lick with you. And that ain't hot to them. See my point?"

"In most ways," I replied, totally in agreement with Sean's rant.

"I been killing niggas since I was twelve years old. Majority of them niggas I killed was rats. Just like you. You killed your own brother for violating the code. How gangsta is that? That proves that you believe in the Omerta and the code that says 'No Snitching Allowed'. These young niggas have redefined the code, young'un. Changed it to fit whatever narrative they want. Feel me? The code is what it is and should never be tampered with. The code is this: you become a rat when you debrief, make statements implicating others, verbal, written, or videotaped. Signing affidavits implicating people in crimes that can send them to jail. Setting niggas up for the feds, wearing wires, pointing niggas out, getting on the stand and implicating niggas…all that shit is 'hot'. It's the intent. Writing a book and putting shit that's already public knowledge and all the niggas involved are dead isn't hot. But let these niggas today tell it, it is. Shit twisted…" Sean's phone vibrated suddenly. He looked at the phone and then the rearview mirror. "About time." Sean turned to me. "Here's how we get to Kenny Sparrow, right here."

Before I could say a word, a woman walked up to the caravan on the driver's side. Sean let the window down. "Trina, what's up, baby girl?"

The woman was stylishly dressed, but she wasn't that good-looking. She leaned into the window and hugged Sean. "Can't believe they finally let your ass out of jail. Welcome home, Sean."

"Thanks. I'm definitely glad to be home," Sean said and reached into his pocket. He pulled out a wad of money and passed it through the window to the woman. "Order some food in front of him. I'ma bring the food to the door. You let us in, then bounce. You know the routine."

"Just like old time, huh? You ain't gon' never change."

"I'm too old to change, Trina."

"I heard that. Look, I ain't gon' be but about twenty minutes once I get up there. He's expecting me. Kenny's dick game is garbage. He gon' bust quick and be ready to sleep. He lives on the sixth floor in apartment 614. Be ready when I text you," Trina said.

"Got it," Sean replied.

"Good. See y'all in a few."

Trina turned and crossed the street. We watched her go to the entrance of the building and get buzzed in.

"You trust her, slim?" I asked Sean. "I mean, can she be trusted not to tell after the cops find her prints in there after Kenny's dead?"

Sean smiled at me. "You don't know who that is, do you?"

"You called her Trina, so I guess that must be Trina."

"That just ain't any old Trina, young'un. That's Trinaboo."

Anthony Fields

I had heard a lot about the notorious Trinaboo. The woman was legendary in the streets of D.C. for a whole lot of reasons. "Oh yeah? So, her name and reputation make her trustworthy?"

"Naw, Que. What makes a woman like Trinaboo trustworthy is knowledge and fear. Trina knows that if she crosses me once, her daughter Tiera gon' die. And her son, li'l Mike. She knows that I'ma kill everybody in her whole family if she talks. Her fear of me will keep her quiet. Trina knows me. Know exactly what I do. What I been doing for years. That makes her trustworthy."

"Muthafuckas be saying that she got that HIV shit."

"Niggas been saying that for years. She still here. Besides, you can't tell my man Tim Tim that shit."

"Tim Tim?"

"Yeah, my man Timothy Doyle from Uptown. He fucking with her right now. He loves her. Just another tender dick nigga like you," Sean said and chuckled.

"Stop playing with me, old head. I told you that earlier."

"A'ight, whatever. But listen, I need you to not just hear me but to feel me on what I was saying to you earlier. The code has been rewritten by lesser men, by kids and half way grown men who think that fuckin' transgendered niggas is cool because they got titties. Hot shit nowadays is being defined by fuck boys and rats."

"Rats?"

"You fuckin' right. Rats are telling real niggas what's hot and what's not and not the other way around. Like I said, shit is twisted. Beefing with niggas is ninety percent verbal now. If niggas get mad at you for whatever reason, the first thing they tell niggas is that you hot. If you fuck your co-defendant's baby mother and he finds out, you gon' be hot. If niggas get jealous because you getting too much money, you must be hot. You got the bag and fuck all the bad bitches, you hot. You beat too many cases in court, you hot. If you go in on a beef and get out too quick, you hot. You feel me!"

"I feel you, slim. I feel you."

"Good. Don't forget it."

Chapter 2
ZIN

It took me ten minutes to drive from Georgetown to Adams Morgan. In the parking garage, I looked for Jermaine's Jaguar and didn't see it. I breathed a sigh of relief and exited the Infiniti. A few minutes later, I was turning the doorknob and entering the condo. To my surprise, there were boxes everywhere that lined the living room and bedroom. Apparently, Jermaine was moving out as well. I noticed that several of the boxes were marked. They had Zin written on them with black marker. Those boxes totaled seven. One box was my stuff from the office that Nikki Locks had dropped off. The others were clothes, shoes, and toiletries.

There was one box in particular that got my attention. This box didn't have my name on it and it was different from all the others. I recognized it instantly. This one box was a box that had been in storage before I moved into the condo with Jermaine. It was a box of things that belonged to my mother. I'd been contacted by the storage company years ago and told to come and get the contents of storage unit nine because the lease was up. No one had come to renew the contract in months. I remembered driving to the storage facility to retrieve the boxes. The main stuff I took to my aunt's house and stored them in her basement. But one box I took to the condo to go through at a later date. That date never came and I never got around to see what was in the box. Until now. I pulled up a chair and sat down in front of the box.

I opened the box and pulled out pieces of clothing, then fingered the fabric, trying to remember my mother wearing it. I couldn't, but I could still see Patricia Carter's face. My mother was radiant, elegant, and beautiful. Her posture and demeanor made it hard to believe that she had been born and raised in D.C.'s harshest ghettos in Southeast. She spoke as if she had attended the finest academics the nation had to offer, but she never even graduated high school. I fingered the locket attached to the chain around my neck. It held my mother's picture. I felt myself getting nostalgic and emotional.

Anthony Fields

There were several small boxes inside the one big box. Each box contained a separate piece of my mother. One box held shoes. Suede Gucci heels that were a perfect size seven, just like my own. I extracted two shoes from the box and set them down on the floor. I undid the clasps on my Michael Kors opened toed pumps and peeled them off one by one. Then I slipped my feet into my mother's shoes. They were a perfect fit. I stood and walked around the condo and suddenly I felt closer to my mother. Of all the shoes that she had, I wondered why she'd chosen to keep these shoes put up. I went back to the box and pulled out a gown. It was a white beaded, lace Chanel dress that I guessed had to have been my mother's wedding dress. Tears formed in my eyes as I fingered the dress and imagined her wearing it. Inside the box was a small jewelry box - and a shoebox filled with papers. Inside the jewelry box was a gold chain and charm that had the letters P and C hanging from it. I walked over to the dresser and put the chain on. It fell loosely around my neck.

"Why have I never checked these boxes before?" I asked myself. Back at the box, I pulled out the shoebox of papers. I rifted through the papers and found my mother's license, Social Security card, voter registration card, and several credit cards. The credit cards were for stores that were no longer in business like Hechts, Woodward & Lothrop, and Montgomery Ward. There were photos of me as a baby, me as a kid up until my mother's death, and several pictures of her and my father together. They looked to be happy in each photo, and they made a beautiful couple. I smiled as I remembered how much they seemed to love each other.

There was a small manila envelope amongst the papers. I turned it over in my hand and noticed that it was sealed. The envelope bore no markings. I shook it and held it up to the light to see if I could see inside of it. I couldn't. I used one of the keys on my key ring to tip the envelope and then tear it along the top. Inside the envelope were several pieces of paper, the type of yellow paper that was sold as a legal pad. I pulled two papers out of the envelope and unfolded them. There was writing on most of the pages, front and back. I recognized my mother's handwriting immediately. Her cursive was fluent and legible, unmistakable. The pages totaled four altogether. I started from the first page and read. The words were my mother's words that obviously she'd written to someone, or herself. I couldn't be sure...

Things grow progressively worse each day now. Our relationship has changed drastically in the last year or so. The way that he looks at me, touches me, it's all so foreign to me. It's as if I'm living with a stranger. Gone is the loving way that he'd touch me. Sex is bestial and degrading. I feel as if I am his whore instead of his wife. I believe that he knows. He has to. That is the only explanation for the cold look in his eyes and the distance between us. I feel like a prisoner in my own home at times. And my husband is my jailer. The way he watches me ... it's spooky. When he's home, it's as if he's far away and when he's far away, it's as if he's here. Staring at me, accusing me. Is it possible that he could see the stain of betrayal in my eyes? In my heart? Is love really that powerful? I cry myself to sleep at night and pray that our daughter doesn't hear me. My sweet precious daughter. I love her, so and so does he. Without her, I'd go crazy. Cooking, cleaning, and caring for Zin is my perpetual nirvana. Her smile, her voice, her laugh, it comforts me.

I paused to wipe the tears from my eyes. It was as if I could hear my mother speaking from the grave.

It's been four years since Ameen's death and I still feel his absence, his loss. I know that having an affair with my husband's best friend was dangerous and wrong. But the man was like forbidden fruit that I had to taste. His body, his demeanor, his sex appeal, his light grey eyes. They were too much for me to resist. I believe that my husband knows of my infidelity. He knows, and he's mentally punishing me. The last night of my lover's life, as we made love in my bed while my husband was away, I heard a noise in the house. But I dismissed it that night as one of things that go bump in the night. I was too caught up in that act of betrayal to think clearly. Too much in the throes of passion to get up and investigate the sounds that I heard. But as sure as I sit here and write this down on paper, I know what I heard. I now believe that my husband was here that night. He was here and he saw us. I may be delusional or I may just be paranoid, I don't know. I believe that my husband saw us and that he killed my lover as a result of what he saw. These are words I can never speak to a soul, so I must write them down, to get them out of my head, my heart, my soul. As sure as I write this today, I know that Mike killed Ameen. No one could get that close to Ameen Bashir but someone he knew. Someone he trusted. Mike. I also believe that one day soon, he's going to kill me. I can feel it. People say that before you die, your whole life flashes before your eyes. I took that to mean that it flashed before your eyes at the moment of your death. But now I know different. Your life flashes before your eyes in stages, and you can feel that death is near. I feel that now.

My husband has taken to disrespecting me publicly. He brings the reminder of my betrayal to our house from time to time. Every time I see Ameen's son, Quran, I think of his father and our infidelity. Quran has a friend named Dontay, and they ride with Mike everywhere. They kill people for Mike. That I know for sure and for some reason, I believe that they will kill me. It's in their eyes. Their young, teenaged eyes. The way they look at me. When I die – and I believe that I will die soon – my husband and his young assassins will be my executioners. I won't miss my life as it is now, but I will miss my daughter. Zin is the only thing good and pure in my life, and I love her with all my heart.

My heart stopped momentarily as I recorded to memory my mother's words. Tears fell from my eyes by the twos and threes. My soul was devastated, my mind befogged. All I could do was shake my head in disbelief as the papers fell from my hand. It couldn't be. What my mother wrote couldn't be true! I picked up the papers and read them again through tear filled eyes. I stopped at the mention of Quran's name. Not only had Quran known my father, but he also knew my mother. He had met her, seen her on several occasions, and he neglected to tell me that as well. Suddenly I realized that a lot of what Quran had told me was lies. Reading the next line again made my hands shake.

If You Cross Me Once 2

Quran has a friend named Dontay, and they ride with Mike everywhere. They kill people for Mike. That I know for sure and for some reason, I believe that they will kill me.

My cries turned into ear piercing screams, as I realized that my mother had predicted her own death, and she had even predicted who her killers would be. And she was right. I dropped to my knees and buried my face in my hands. I had been lied to, tricked, and deceived, by my father and by the man that I loved. My father was behind my mother's murder, her rape, her beating. She was killed for an act of betrayal. Infidelity. Killed by Dontay Samuels and Quran Bashir. I slowly rose to my feet and wiped my nose and eyes. I wanted justice for my mother. I wanted revenge. I paced back and forth in the living room thinking, plotting, and planning.

"The one thing you have to do, Zin," my inner voice said, "is not wear your emotions on your sleeve. Never let anyone, especially your father or Quran, know how you truly feel. Be like a chess master and play the pieces on the board the way you are supposed to. Be smart. Be cunning. Calculated. Precise. And you'll reach your goal…"

With a renewed sense of purpose, I stepped out of the Gucci shoes that once belonged to my mother and put my heels back on. I took off the chain that held my mother's initials and put it back in the jewelry box. The jewelry box went into my purse along with my mother's letter. The shoes went back into the big box. I made a mental note to come back for all the boxes with a bigger vehicle. The one box with my mother's things in it was leaving with me. I lifted the box and left the condo.

Anthony Fields

Chapter 3
QURAN

Sean glanced at his phone, then reached for the door handle. "Showtime, young'un. Let's go."

We exited the caravan and walked across the street to the building where Kenny Sparrow lived. As we approached, the lock on the building door buzzed and clicked. Inside the building's lobby, there was a desk that was unmanned. We found the elevator with no problem. Sean slipped on latex gloves before pressing the button to summon the elevator. I followed suit with the gloves. The inside of the elevator had cameras in it, so Sean and I both pulled our Papa John's pizza hats down low onto our heads and never looked up. Sean pressed the button for the fifth floor. We got off the elevator there, walked a short distance to the stairwell, and ascended the final flight of stairs to the sixth floor. In my hands, I carried two empty pizza boxes. Sean's hands were empty. At condo 614, Sean knocked on the door. Seconds later, the door opened and a fully-clothed Trina-boo appeared.

"He's in the bedroom. No gun that I could see. He's worn out sexually and doesn't suspect anything. He knows I ordered pizza and here we are. My part is done, right?" Trina asked.

Sean never answered Trina. Instead, he pushed her aside and led the way into the condo. As I walked into the condo, Trina walked out. I closed the door and locked it.

"Bring the pizza in here, Trina. I'm hungry as shit," a male voice called out from the bedroom. "What kind did you get?"

We beelined for the room where the voice came from. Sean pulled his silenced pistol. I did the same. There was only one bedroom in the condo. Another door led to a bathroom off the hallway. The bedroom's door was ajar. Sean walked right in with me on his heels.

"Trina ordered your favorite brand of pizza, homie. Cheese."

At the sound of Sean's voice, Kenny Sparrow opened his eyes and sat up in bed. His lower body was covered by the sheet. He quickly reached for something on the floor.

Sean shot Kenny in the back, then walked over and pushed Kenny back onto the bed.

"A-a-r-r-g-g-h-h! What the fuck? Fuck you doing, Sean?" Kenny bellowed.

"Shut the fuck up, you piece of shit."

"Whatever that bitch Tina told you, she lied."

"What Trina told me? Nigga, this ain't about nothing that Trina said. This is about what Reese told me."

"I'm bleeding to death, slim. Fuck you shoot me for?" Kenny asked.

"That little flesh wound in your side is the least of your worries, homie. Trust me."

"I can't believe that bitch set me up."

"Believe it, homie. Today is the day you answer for your sins."

"O-o-o-w-w, this ain't no flesh wound, slim. Get an ambulance. I swear to god, I won't tell nobody who shot me."

Sean laughed. "You swear to God? You won't tell nobody? You funny as shit. But I know you ain't gon' tell nobody I shot you because the next person you meet is gon' be God. Hot, faggie-ass nigga…"

"Sean, c'mon, man… Whatever you think I did, I didn't do it, slim! I swear to God, I didn't. I know you just came home. If it's money you need, I got you. Don't do no goofy shit and kill me for no reason. Don't let me die for something I didn't do. Take the money, slim, and I'll get to a hospital on my own."

Sean shook his head. "Sorry, Kenny, no can do. I don't care what your mouth says. You're guilty to me. Ain't no amount of money gon' save you."

"Big homie," I intervened, "hear him out. What type of money is he talking about giving you?"

"How much money you got, Kenny? How much is your life worth?" Sean asked.

Kenny's eyes shined with relief at a possible reprieve. "I got almost a half a mill in here and another half in another spot out in Virginia. That's almost a whole mill, slim. Perfect for a man just coming home. Forget about whatever it is you think I did and take

If You Cross Me Once 2

the money. After I get you the money from my VA spot, I'm gone, you'll never see me again."

"Where's the money at? The money you got in here?"

"In the closet over there. Behind the stacked-up boxes of shoes is a bigger box. The box that the flat screen and surround sound came in. the money is in that box."

"Check it out, Que. See if the money is really there."

The large box was exactly where Kenny said it would be. I opened the box. It was filled with cash. "Jackpot," I whispered to myself. Exiting the closet, I told Sean, "It's in there, slim. I'm not sure if it the amount he said it was, but the box is filled with cash."

"Cool. Go and find something to put the money in." Sean ordered. "Check one of the hall closets for some pillowcases. In the meantime, I need to talk with Kenny a little while longer."

I left the room and searched the hall closets until I found exactly what I was looking for. I grabbed a handful of pillowcases and went back to the bedroom.

"...lied to you, slim." Kenny was saying. "I never gave Reese shit. Why would I pay him to say that you killed Raymond? We all saw Mike Carter kill Raymond."

"I don't have a clue."

"But think about it. Fuck I get a key of coke from back then? A whole brick that I'ma just give a nigga to lie on another nigga. To get him out the way? That shit don't even make sense. It wouldn't have taken Reese's crack smoking ass to be given no brick to lie. And you know that. Plus, you know me back then. I wasn't getting that type of money then. Where the fuck I get a brick to give away? I don't know why Reese lied to you, but on my mother's grave, he lied. I didn't have shit to do with what happened with you back in the day. You gotta believe me, slim."

"I believe you, slim. For some strange reason, I believe you."

"I'm telling you the truth, slim. Bullshit ain't nothing."

Sean pulled out a roll of duct tape. "I believe you, but I still gotta secure you. At least until I get that other money from the spot at VA. When I get the money, I'll let you go free and clear." Sean duct taped Kenny's legs and wrists. Then he left the room.

Anthony Fields

Our move on Kenny wasn't scripted, so I had no idea what Sean was about to do next. He reentered the room moments later with a couple different knives in his hands. Kenny's eyes grew large with fear and sheer terror. "Come on, Sean, you said…"

"I know what I said, homie. These knives are to cut the tape off after we get the rest of the money. Just chill out. As a matter of fact…" Sean dropped the kitchen knives on the bed and grabbed the duct tape. He pulled off a strip and put it across Kenny's mouth. He instantly started to make muffled noises. Sean cuffed the tape and picked up the knives. "Which one of these joints do you think is best for carving?" Sean asked me.

"Carving? The joint with the black handle and deep serrated ridges."

"That's what I thought, too, but I couldn't be sure. Great minds think alike, Que. That's why I fuck with you, young'un."

"Fuck you about to carve?" I asked Sean.

"Him," Sean said and nodded at Kenny.

"But what about the rest of the money?"

"Fuck the rest of the money."

"I thought you said you believed what he said about not being the one who paid Reese to lie on you?"

"I do believe him. But that ain't gon' stop me from killing him. Even if he didn't put Reese up to tell on me, he's still guilty. Kenny made statements on the R Street case and on my man Kenny. And you already know what we do to rats."

"Kill 'em."

"Exactly." Sean walked over to the bed as Kenny squirmed like a fish on a hook. He plunged the knife into Kenny repeatedly until he stopped squirming. Then he hopped up onto the bed. He positioned himself to stand behind Kenny, but over him. Sean lifted Kenny's head with one hand, with his other hand, he stuck the knife in Kenny's neck and started to cut in a sawing motion. Blood coated his hands, clothes, and the bedsheets.

I stood in my spot and watched Sean completely sever Kenny Sparrow's head. The scene was straight out of a horror movie. Sean stood on the bed, covered in blood, a kitchen knife in one hand and Kenny's severed head in the other hand.

Sean climbed off the bed. "I need to get this rat's blood off of me and change out of these clothes, so I'ma hop in the shower and find something to put on in here. Get all the money out of the box and put it in the pillowcases." Sean dropped the head and the knife and walked out of the room.

I couldn't believe what I had just witnessed. Sean Branch was a certified lunatic. I'd been watching him kill since I was fourteen years old, but I had never seen such butchery and savagery by him. Shooting people was one thing, but chopping off heads was a whole different form of lunching. Dealing with Sean, you never knew what you were gonna get from him. One day we were burying bodies in shallow graves, the next he was in an expensive condo in upper Northwest cutting off heads.

I walked into the closet and did what Sean asked me to do. I filled the pillowcases up with the cash from the box, all the while, thinking about the other half of a million dollars that we'd be leaving behind. By the time I finished filling up four pillowcases with money, Sean was entering the room draped in nothing but a towel. I dropped all four pillowcases by the bed. "I'ma let you get dressed, big homie. Call me once you're dressed."

Fifteen minutes later, Sean called me into the room. The clothes he had on were visibly too big, but he made it work. "You ready to bounce?"

"Yeah, I had to wipe down everything." Sean said as he dropped the two knives he'd touched into a pillowcase. The clothes that he'd worn into the condo followed. "Hey, Que, grab that head for me and toss it to me."

"Slim, I ain't touching that fuckin' head."

"Scary-ass nigga," Sean said and walked over to Kenny's severed head. He picked it up and put it in the pillowcase with the clothes, knives and duct tape.

"Scared of a little head."

"You lunchin' like shit, big homie."

"Naw, you lunchin'. Grab them bags with the money in 'em and let's get the fuck outta here."

***

In the caravan, I asked Sean, "Fuck you gon' do with that stupid-ass head?"

"I haven't really decided yet. I just took it because I always fantasized about doing it. Always wanted to cut a rat nigga's head off. Just happened to be Kenny's."

"I'm sorry to hear that, slim. That's how Jeffrey Dahmer and them niggas got started on their serial killer shit."

Sean laughed at that. "Young'un, you fucked up in the head just as much as me."

"How you figure that? I ain't riding around with dead bodies in the whip or cutting off heads riding with 'em"

"That part might be true, but look at what you just said about Jeffrey Dahmer. Nigga, you and I are serial killers. Dahmer did a rack of wild shit to his victims, but guess what? You've killed more niggas then Jeffrey Dahmer did. So have I. That nigga ain't got shit on us. Think about it."

I thought about what Sean said. "Yeah, I guess you're right."

"I know I'm right. But on another note, speaking of Kenny's head, he never did have much brains. He wasn't smart enough to put that type of play against me together. And something he said to me back there won't leave my head."

"Which part?"

Sean drove in silence for a few minutes, then he said, "When he said that he wasn't getting no money back then and that he didn't have no key of coke to give away. He wasn't lying about that. When Reese said that, I never paid that part any mind until now. So, Reese lied on Kenny, and I can't figure out why. He was about to die and he knew it, but still he lied. Why? He had to be afraid of whoever he was lying to protect. Who in the hell scared him that much? To protect them even in death?"

"Good question, slim. But ones that I can't answer."

"Neither can I. I always been like the boogeyman to niggas in the street, but yet Reese lied to me for somebody. Somebody that he fears more than me." Sean got quiet again. Then he laughed. "I just thought about something your father told me."

"My father?" I repeated with confusion in my face. "You know my father?"

"Of course I knew your father. He's the one that introduced me to Mike."

"You never mentioned that to me before. Why?"

Sean stared straight ahead. "No reason. I just assumed that you knew that."

"I didn't. I never knew that you knew my father."

"Well, I did. He's the reason I am what I am today. Let me finish what I was saying, and then I'll tell you how I met your father."

Anthony Fields

Chapter 4
SEAN BRANCH

"You said we got another stop to make, right?" Quran asked me.

"Yeah, on Third Street, right off of Livingston Road. That's where I'm headed to."

"A'ight. I got some other shit I gotta do, but it's cool."

"I can drop you off if you need me to. I can handle this next situation by myself."

"Naw, I'm good. I'm with you. Finish what you were saying."

"Your father told me to always crush those who seek to harm you. But if you don't see the harm coming, you can't crush foes you know nothing about. So, always know your enemies. He told me to never waver and never show mercy. Anyone that crosses you, he said, must know that they are gambling with their lives and that they will lose. That they will die. He stressed to me that dudes in the streets only respect strength that is greater than theirs and men who go harder than them. And above all else, they respect——"

"Killers," Quran said, finishing my sentence. "Killers with success at defeating their enemies."

I nodded my head. "Correct. If you are betrayed or crossed by anyone, let that slight be their last. Because if someone crosses you once, they will cross you twice. That was one of the last things Ameen told me before he was killed."

"He told me the same things. I instilled it in my brothers. Jihad remembered it. Khitab didn't. That's why he's no longer with us."

I thought about Quran's younger brother, Khitab. Then I thought about what Quran had done to him. He'd described the whole murder to me one day. I'd only seen Khitab Bashir one time. He had been a small kid back then, maybe about six or seven years old. To kill one's own brother is something that most people couldn't do. But Quran had done it. I admired that in him.

I continued what I remembered his father had told me. "Anyone - and I mean anyone who crosses you - must know that their life is forfeit. Kenny Sparrow knew that and violated the codes anyway. What I just did to him was planned, but it was strategic. When the streets find out that he was found dead missing his head, the whispers will begin. Niggas will eventually figure out that it was me who did the killing. Taking the head was for maximum effect. Now, the streets will know that Sean Branch is back, and it sends a message to other rats that they need to be very afraid because the Grim Reaper is coming."

"A'ight, Mr. Grim Reaper is coming. But the rats already getting that message. I been sending that message for years. And all that's cool, but I'ma need you to get back to you knowing my father and never telling me that."

"To be honest with you, Que, I don't know why I never told you that. It just never came up before. Wasn't no secret. Everybody in the streets knew that Ameen Bashir was my mentor. I wouldn't have mentioned it today had I not heard his voice in my head telling me all the stuff he embedded in me as a young nigga when you and I met all them years ago, I assumed that Mike had already told you that your father groomed me."

"He didn't. And I wonder why?" Quran stated.

I shrugged my shoulders. "I don't know then, young'un. I assumed he did. Mike knows the relationship between me and Ameen. I figured it was the reason why he linked us together. Anyway, young'un, your father was my idol. He was a real street legend. There should be books written about him. Nobody was fuckin' with Ameen Bashir on any level back in the day. He was loved, feared, and respected. Your father was like a father to me, and not just because he was fuckin' my mother."

"Fuckin' your mother?" Quran repeated and laughed. "Stop what you doing, old head. My father never cheated on Sister Khadijah. He loved her too much."

I turned to Quran and looked him in the eyes. "Have I ever lied to you? Ever shot you some bullshit disguised as law?"

"Naw. Not that I know of. It's just that…"

"Look, young'un, that's your pops and your mother, may they both rest in peace. I get that. After all these years of thinking one thing, it's hard finding out something different. But the truth is, your father was a rolling stone. Wherever he laid his hat was home.

If You Cross Me Once 2

Women couldn't resist him. The color of his eyes hooked them every time. I know because my mother and your father argued constantly about all the other chicks he was hitting besides her and his wife. I always knew who your father was in regards to women, but it wasn't my place to have that conversation with you. Until now. Your father's been gone twenty years. You're grown now, and you can handle the truth better. You have to be able to accept certain truths even if you don't want to. I had to do that when I realized that your father didn't really give two fucks about my mother. To him, she was just pussy. As a teenager, I realized that and had to accept it.

"At first, I thought that your father loved my mother. But over time, I learned different. I was like ten when your father started messing with my mother. My father was a killer, too. He passed that gene down to me. Just as your father gave the gift to you. My father got locked up for killing two people in a park near Chillum Road. He got a rack of time out Maryland and ended up getting stabbed to death in the Cut Annex Penitentiary. That fucked my mother up and set the stage for your father to slide in. He spent a lot of time at my house. He raised me into the man that I am today. Your father put a gun in my hand, just like he put one in yours. Ameen Bashir harnessed my emotions and made me heartless."

"Damn, slim!" Quran said. "That's crazy!"

"I already know. Your father sent me on missions to kill as soon as I turned twelve."

"The same way that Mike Carter did me."

I nodded in agreement with Quran. "Our stories are too similar, huh? I'm already hip. I killed a lot of people for your father, but there was one that he was most proud of. The victim was a man named Lonnell Gamble. He owed Mike money for drugs and refused to pay. Mike Carter put Ameen on the dude. Your father put me on him. Lonnell Gamble did business out of his girlfriend's beauty salon. Had a crew of killers around him at all times. Nigga thought that he was untouchable. Kid killers were totally unheard of back then. Ameen dressed me in a private school uniform and sent me into the salon. I walked into the salon and asked for Lonnell

Gamble. Nobody paid me any mind. I was directed to an office in the rear of the salon. As I walked down the hallway in the back, I slipped into the bathroom and screwed the silencer attachment onto the Taurus. Lonnell Gamble was sitting behind a desk talking on the phone when I walked in. He looked up and saw me…"

"What's up, li'l man?" he said as he pulled the phone away from his ear.

"You should've just paid the money," I replied, I aimed the gun and shot the man several times in the head and chest.

"Then I just walked out of the salon. I smiled and said goodbye to all the women in the booths getting their hair done. One of the women said, 'His li'l ass gon' be fine as shit when he grows up.'

"Your father picked me up on Eighth Street around the corner. After that, I became arrogant. I turned into an animal and became ferocious. I became the lion in the jungle and everybody else became prey. Whoever Ameen told me to kill, I killed. No questions asked. I wasn't even making a lot of money. Your father gave me drugs that he got from Mike Carter, and he gave me a little money, never much. But he kept me fly, and I was cool with that. At some point, he introduced me to Mike Carter. After your father got killed, I was a wild beast on the loose, with no direction, no purpose. I killed dudes for no good reason. Then one day, Mike Carter showed up at my house. He gave me fifty racks and asked me to take over where your father left off. That's how I ended up working for him. A year or two later, he introduced me to you. The day we killed Curtbone and Rick Love n'em."

"I remember that day like it was yesterday. When I first saw you, I thought you was a migo." Quran said and smiled.

I laughed. "A migo, huh? How the fuck you gon' think I was a migo and your ass got the same dark, curly hair and fuckin' grey eyes? Fuck you got in you? White people?"

"We all got the slave master's blood in us, nigga. Don't try and act like you don't."

"True dat. But your great grandmother's pussy was torch because massa got them pretty-ass light grey eyes in y'all bloodline."

If You Cross Me Once 2

"Oh yeah? You gon' play with Great Grams like that? Fuck you, nigga."

"Naw. I keep telling you. Fuck with me."

Quran turned around and glanced into the back seat. "Either my mind is playing tricks on me or I swear, I can smell that head."

"Your mind is playing tricks on you. It's too early to smell it. Dudes in the streets only respect strength that's greater than theirs. That head is my strength."

"Yeah, a'ight, whatever. But on some real shit, big homie, I glad that you mentioned my father and told me your story. Even if it opens my eyes and changes the image I had of him all my life. I can definitely see him being a ladies' man, though, and the apple don't fall far from the tree."

"So says the guy who just met Zin Carter and fell in love already. But go ahead, tender dick, what was you saying?"

"I was saying I needed to hear something about my father. He meant the world to me, to my family, and sometimes I forget him. Ameen Bashier was a great man. He should never be forgotten. If he was here, my brother would have never pulled that rat shit and I wouldn't have had to kill him. Somebody took my father away from us, and I wish I knew who it was so that I could kill his entire family. Real talk.

"I feel you, young'un. I feel you."

***

I glanced at the address texted to my phone and then looked at the numbers on the last house on Third Street. 620. The addresses were the same. The house was a red brick, two-story home just like the ones that lined both sides of Third Street. I pulled onto the block in an open parking spot. "This is where we're going, Que. C'mon." I got out of the caravan and went into the backseat. Grabbing a bundle of money, I pocketed it and shut the rear door.

Quran followed me up the street and into the gate that surrounded the house. The door to the house opened as we approached it.

James "Doo Doo" Yarborough pulled the door all the way open. "Glad that you could finally make it. Who dis? And fuck you got on those big ass clothes for?"

"This is my man Quran. Quran, this is Doo Doo," I said as we entered the house.

"What's up?" Quran said to Doo Doo.

"Sup. Your man is in the living room all tied up," Doo Doo announced.

Doo Doo led the way through the house until we reached the living room. There was a man seated on the couch. He had a Hugo Boss headband stretched around his head. His beard was long and well-trimmed. I let my attention fall on the man lying on the living room floor. His feet were tied at the ankles, his wrists tied together behind his back. The man's mouth was taped up. He squirmed around and tried to speak, but his words were muffled by the tape over his mouth.

"This is my man, Whistle, Sean. He's the one who got him here."

"Que, the man over there tied up is a takeout rat named Crud. He jumped on my man's case and cooked him in trial last year. I was in Colorado fucked up about my man blowing trial. This muthafucka was the only street nigga to testify. Bitch nigga told the jury that he bought heroin from my man's and n'em every three days for a year, and guess what?"

"What?" Quran asked.

"My man didn't even know this nigga. He was introduced to them by..." I turned and pointed at the man seated on the couch. "That nigga."

"Aye, slim..." the man named Whistle started as he moved.

Quran pulled his pistol immediately. "Aye, slim, what? Move again and I'ma crush your ass."

"Sean," Doo Doo said, confused. "What's all this about?"

"You did me a favor, is what this is about. You saved me the trouble of having to find this nigga next. His name is Artinis Wiston, right?" I asked Doo Doo.

If You Cross Me Once 2

Doo Doo looked at his man seated on the couch. He nodded his head.

"The look on your face tells me that you didn't… Well, you don't know what's up with your man. Your man Whistle is the one who introduced Crud to Lacy and Buck. The crazy part is that he told them that Crud was a booster who could get designer clothes and shoes dirt cheap. My man n'em never did any business with Crud. Never. The ATF was investigating Lacy, Buck, and some other niggas who hung in the barbershop on MLK. They ended up going in on a conspiracy. Your man Whistle was picked up on that case…"

"He told me that he went in on something else," Doo Doo said, eyes still on his man, Whistle.

"He made statements on the case," I continued. "He never got on the stand…"

"Ain't nobody got no paperwork on me!" Whistle shouted. He looked at Quran, who was a few feet away from him with his silenced gun aimed at him. "That shit ain't true."

"It ain't true, huh? I hear you, slim. Que, stay right there. Doo Doo, I'll be right back. Gotta get something out of the car," I said and left the house.

I walked back to the Dodge and retrieved the knife from the pillowcase with Kenny's head in it. I dumped one pillowcase of money out onto the seat and put the knife in it. I whistled to myself the entire time I walked back to the house on Third. Inside the house, I pulled the knife out. With the gun in one hand and the knife in the other, I approached Byron "Crud" Clark.

"Crud was at D.C. jail on his own charges. He went on a visit to see his lawyer. He came back from that visit and asked Buck to read his discovery. Crud didn't know what was in the discovery packet: the statements that he made on Whistle." I turned back to the man on the couch. "You didn't know that, did you? Crud was gonna tell on you. But Buck saw the statements and confronted Crud with them. Crud checked out of the unit at the jail. From the P.C. block, he contacted the government, and jumped on Lacy and Buck's case. Ain't that right, Crud?"

I peeled back the tape from Crud's mouth.

"Please... please...let me explain what happened!" Crud exclaimed.

"No need," I said, tiring of the whole scene. I shot Crud in the face and head twice, killing him. Then I stood over him, pulled his bloody head back, plunged the knife into his neck and cot. Minutes later, I stood with the gun in one hand and Crud's head in the other. The knife lay on the carpet. The living room was deathly quiet. I looked at the faces of the men in the room. Only Quran looked unfazed by what I'd done. "That's how you kill gangsta rats."

Quran looked at me and nodded his head at Whistle. I smiled and nodded back. Quran shot Whistle in the head.

"You cuttin' his head off, too?" Quran asked.

"Naw, that rat can keep his head for the statements he made. I'll just settle for his tongue."

Setting the severed head down, I picked the knife back up. At the couch, I opened Whistle's mouth and pulled his tongue as far as it would go, then I cut it off. I put the tongue, Crud's head, and the knife in the pillowcase.

"Bruh, here you go with this shit again," Quran said. "Leave that head here."

"Never that, young'un. You know what they say: two heads are better than one. Doo Doo, where's the bathroom? I need to clean up." I pulled out the wad of money and tossed it to Doo Doo. The look on Doo Doo's face was priceless. He seemed to be in shock. "The bathroom, Ock. Where is it?"

"Huh? Bathroom? Uh...it's one around the corner before you get to the kitchen."

"A'ight. When we leave, I want you to douse the house. Torch it. The fire will destroy anything that we left behind. You got that?"

"Got it, slim," Doo Doo replied. "I got it."

***

"One of those pillowcases with money in it is yours. Take it," I told Quran as he exited the Dodge Journey on Howard Road.

The rear door opened and I could hear Quran as he grabbed the pillowcase.

"As always, I appreciate you, big homie."

"That ain't nothing, young'un. You deserve that. It's on Kenny. Killing Crud was premeditated. I kept a promise to a good man by doing that. You killing Whistle was a gift. A bonus of sorts. In the next coming days, I got a lot I need to do. Lives I need to take."

"I can dig that. But can I ask you a question?" Quran asked.

"Ask me anything, Ock," I replied.

"Your baby mother, Raquel. They found her down by the Wharf, floating in the water, disemboweled and shit. I remember how much you talked about her. Loved her. Why did you kill her?"

"I know that you said that you love Zin Carter. Time will reveal if that love is real or not. But have you ever been in love? I mean, really in love? The kind of love where nothing exists but it?"

Quran paused to think, then he replied, "Naw. I can't really say that I have."

"Well, if you ever find that type of love and the person that you love treats you the way Raq treated me while I was in prison, you'll understand. Does that answer your question?"

"I guess so. Another question. Have you talked to Mike Carter since you been home?"

"No, not yet. I'll get around to hollering at him soon."

"Does Zin know that you did the eighteen years in prison for a murder her father committed?"

"I never told her if you didn't."

Quran lifted the pillowcase and swung it over his shoulder. "I didn't. And I was just wondering how much about you she really knows."

"Not much, young boy Que, and I'd prefer that it stays like that."

"All the secrets are safe with me, big homie. Love you, slim."

"Love you too, young'un. I'll be in touch."

***

Anthony Fields

Bolivia "Liv" Santos was the woman who'd held me down all the years that I was in prison. We went to junior high school together and I never paid her any mind. When I got sent to Lorton Correctional Complex after I got sentenced, she came to visit me and never left my side.

I pulled the caravan into the driveway of her townhouse in Alexandria, Virginia. I sat back and replayed everything that Reese and Kenny had said before they died. Kenny denied everything I said, but Reese didn't. Reese confessed his sins, and yet he lied. As he stared the Grim Reaper in the face, he lied to protect someone's secret, someone who scared him more than me, and I believe that I knew who that person is. There's only one person that I know who could instill that type of fear in men like Reese. Michael Carter. And Mike was the only person back then who had a key of coke to give away. Suddenly the answers to the questions that had been in my head for years came to me clearly. Raymond Watson robbed all of Mike Carter's workers in Brentwood. Mike took it personal.

I was in the car with Mike one day when he saw Raymond on Twelfth Street. Raymond was with Reese, standing near a corner store. In a fit of rage, Mike hopped out of the Benz and killed Raymond. A couple weeks later, I was arrested for Raymond's murder. Reese ended up being the eyewitness against me, and Mike never had him killed. He could have put Quran on Reese, but he didn't, and I never understood why until now. Somewhere along the way, Mike decided to kill two birds with one stone. I know all the secrets that Mike kept, so I'd become a threat to him. Instead of killing me, he sent me to jail. He was the one who'd given Reese the brick of coke to implicate me. He got the heat off of himself as well. The move was Machiavellian and vintage Mike Carter. Getting me out of the way also achieved another purpose. I grew too close to Quran and with me gone, I couldn't tell Quran what Mike didn't want him to know - that being that Mike Carter was the one who killed his father.

Chapter 5
BRION "BLAST" CLARK
Temple Hills, MD
11:37 p.m.

"There's something in this liquor / the air is getting thicker / I can't help but stare at you / (oh yeah) girl, what did you do? / (to me) what did you slip up in my cup / 'cause / I want you / I had a little bit too much, girl / so come over here / there's something in this liquor / the air is getting thicker / and all I want is you..."

Renaissance Tyler was a bad bitch on every level, and the whole city knew it. Men and women vied for her attention every day, but she rebuffed them all. Ren Tyler belonged to me. I sat on her bed and watched her dance naked to the Chris Brown song playing on her phone. Her exotic skin tone accented her long hair, which was dyed ruby red. Ren's body was heavily tattooed, but the one that caught my attention the most was my name tattooed across her pelvis, right above her pussy. The curtains were open, which allowed the moonlight to reflect off of the platinum jewelry pierced into Ren's nipples, navel, and clit. As the song gave way to another, Ren walked over and pushed me down onto the bed. She pushed my T-shirt up to reveal my abs. She ran her hand up and down my stomach before undoing my Gucci belt. I lifted myself to allow Ren to remove my jeans. She untied my high-top Gucci tennis shoes and pulled them off one by one, then pulled my jeans all the way off.

From her position on her knees, Ren said, "Take your shirt off. I wanna see my name you got tattooed across your chest."

I took my T-shirt off for her. Ren looked at her name on me, then grabbed my dick and held it.

"Look at me while I do this." She said, "Don't take your eyes off of me."

I did as she said. I laid back on the bed and put my hands beneath my head. I eyed Ren as she put me in her mouth and sucked me. Her eyes were on mine the entire time until I came in her mouth. Ren never missed a beat. She swallowed every drop of my seed while I watched her. After that, she climbed on the bed and stood over me.

"Nobody will ever love you like me." I heard Ren say over the music playing. "Nobody. And don't you ever forget that."

Ren moved up my body and sat her wet pussy on my lips. She moaned as my tongue flicked out and moved inside her. I ate Ren's pussy like it was Thanksgiving and at the time, I was definitely thankful for the love and sex she was giving me.

"Damn, baby!" Ren moaned.

I stepped up my assault on her pussy and she squirted juices all over my face. My beard and mustache were drenched. Lopping at her juices like a cat at a milk dish, I refused to stop until she'd cum at least two times. Once satisfied that Ren had cum enough, I moved her body from my face. By then, I was fully erect and ready for round two. I got up off the bed and stood. The music on Ren's phone had changed to Miguel.

"…I don't wanna be loved / I don't wanna be loved / I just want a quick fix / up in your mix, miss / send me a wish list / I'll have you addicted / so, mommy come hit this / I don't wanna be loved / I don't wanna be loved / I just want a quickie / no bite marks, no scratches, and no hickies / if you can get with that / mommy, come get with me…"

Grabbing Ren's ankle, I pulled her towards me. I lifted her pretty, pedicured foot and licked her toes, one by one. I could slightly taste the red enamel on her toes, but ignored that. Ren loved it when I paid attention to her feet and I always aimed to please. Then suddenly, I was tired of the foreplay. I reached down beside the bed and found the bottle of cranberry Patron and took a generous swig from the bottle.

"Don't be offended, babe, by what I say. It's just a game and how I play," I sang along with the song. "Pillage and plunder, call me a plumber. Knock on this wood, get rocked by this thunder…" I put the dick in Ren and slow-stroked her. Her pussy was so tight and wet, I had to take breaks from it just so that I wouldn't bust too fast.

If You Cross Me Once 2

Ren's moans drowned out the music, but I could still hear the sound of a phone vibrating on the dresser top. Ren's phone continued to play music, so I knew that the vibrating was mine. My eyes found the digital clock on a nightstand across the room. 12:13 a.m. Something inside me said, "answer your phone", but I couldn't. Ren's pussy felt too good and I couldn't stop fucking it.

***

Ren shook me awake. "Blast! Wake up!!"
"What?" I asked, upset at being disturbed from my sleep.
"Either turn your phone off or answer it. It's been vibrating like crazy for a minute now."
I got up out of the bed and grabbed my phone off the dresser. There were missed calls from my mother and sister. Over thirty of them. "What the fuck?" I mumbled as I dialed my mother's phone.
"Brion?"
"I'm here, Ma. What's up?"
"I need you to come home!" My mother said.
"Ma, did something happen?" I asked her.
"Yes, something happened. It's your brother. Somebody killed him…"
My mother was still talking. I could hear her voice in my ear, but I wasn't catching her words. Or maybe, it was just that I stopped listening after she said, 'It's your brother. Somebody killed him.' I inhaled deeply and exhaled loudly. The pain in my belly rose to my chest. My heart was literally broken. I couldn't speak. I could barely breathe.
"…you need to come home. We need you here."
I mumbled "okay" and then the call ended on my mother's end. I stood there in Ren's bedroom with my phone in my hand, my facial expression one of disbelief.
"Baby, what's up?" Ren asked. "What did your mother say?"
"She told me that my brother's dead. Somebody killed him."

***

Anthony Fields

The drive to Southeast seemed to take forever. Ren glanced in my direction periodically, but kept quiet. She knew me better than anyone in the world. What I needed at the moment was silence. I needed time to accept what I'd been told. That my big brother was gone. Never to return again. I leaned back in my seat and wiped tears from my eyes. My mother had four children, including me. Two girls and two boys. My brother Crud had been the oldest child. Me, I was the third child. My sister Brechelle was the baby. Since our father was a slave to his addiction, my brother had always been our protector, our father figure. He'd taught me how to survive in Ward Eight, D.C.'s most treacherous ward. It was him who had tied my shoes, wiped my eyes when I cried, and fought my battles until I could defend myself. It was my brother who put the first gun in my hand and taught me to shoot. He got me my first piece of pussy, taught me to dress fly, and schooled me to shooting dice and selling drugs. He gave me the nickname Blast after seeing my love for guns and sex. We talked almost every day on the phone. I could still hear his infectious laugh in my head. I could see his face, tattoos all over his bald head, the tattooed teardrop under his right eye. I couldn't believe he was gone.

***

"The police called me from his cell phone," my mother said as she cried. "Said that there had been a fire, but due to the quick response from the neighbors, the fire department got to the house in time to put out the fire before it got too bad. There were two bodies found inside the house - some house on Third Street off of Atlantic Street. They wanted to ID the bodies and notify the next of kin. They found Byron's cell phone in his pocket and his driver's license. He was in their system, since he's been arrested on several occasions. They found my name in his file and my number in his phone. They asked for a birthmark or anything that could verify his identity. I said, 'If y'all got his phone, there's pictures of him in the phone. Compare the photos.' "

And that's when my mother broke down crying.

My sister Bionca walked up and comforted my mother. She turned to me. "They couldn't compare photos because whoever killed Byron cut off his head."

"What?" I exclaimed. "Well, how do they know it's——"

"Him?" Bionca finished my sentence. "Because Mommy told them about the portrait of her Byron had tattooed on his left arm. They looked for it and found it. It's him. Brechelle!" Bionca called out.

My youngest sister walked up, her eyes bloodshot red from crying. "Huh?"

"Take Mommy upstairs and help her undress. Make sure she lies down for a while," Bionca said and gave my mother, distraught with grief, to my sister."

We both stood there and watched my mother and sister disappear up the stairs.

"Did you see the shape that Mommy is in?" Bionca asked me.

"How can I not? I'm standing right here, looking, ain't I?" I replied with an attitude.

"Well, act like you see her then and do something about it. I don't give two fucks about all the wild shit that Crud was into, what he did or who he pissed off. He was my brother. Our brother. And nobody had the right to take him away from us. Did you hear what I just said about what they did to him?"

"I heard you."

"Somebody cut my brother's fuckin' head off." Bionca's voice broke and she started crying. "They decapitated him, Brion!" She paused to allow herself a moment to recover, but she couldn't. Bionca loosed a wail so loud that it chilled me to the bone. She collapsed to the floor and covered her face with her hands. She rocked and cried, rocked and cried.

And there was nothing I could do to comfort her. I was helpless. I stood riveted to my spot and cried like a baby.

Then, as quickly as the fit of pain and rage gripped my sister, it dissipated. She got up off her knees and wiped her eyes. The look in her eyes was one of fire and death. "Somebody killed my brother.

Take your ass out in them streets and find out who did it. Then you kill their ass. Starting with Whistle. He was the last person to call Crud's phone, the police said. He has to know something. Kill him and everybody involved. If you can't do it, then I'm gonna do it. Then I'ma kill your ass. Do you understand me?"

I wiped tears from my eyes and stiffened my resolve. "I understand."

"Good. now, get the fuck out and do what I said. I gotta go and comfort our mother."

Chapter 6
ZIN
The next day…
United States Penitentiary Canaan
Waymart, Pennsylvania

I wore Louis Vuitton flats for comfort. I removed them and my Louis belt before walking up through the metal detector. I put my shoes, belt, and the change bag in the tray.

"Thank you, ma'am. Can you please turn and face the wall?" the female C.O. asked.

I did as I was instructed and was rewarded with an invasive pat search that added to my irritation, but I tucked my feelings away.

"You're good to go, ma'am. Enjoy your visit."

Once I was seated, the thoughts and questions that had fogged my head since yesterday came back full force. I wondered if the slight bags under my eyes would tell the story of how little sleep I'd had since reading my mother's letter. No matter how hard I tried, I couldn't silence the voice in my head. Why hadn't Quran ever mentioned the fact that he not only knew Dontay Samuels, but he'd been close friends with him? Greg Gamble made the case that Dontay Samuels was killed because he had killed my mother. Where did Greg Gamble get that premise from? How could he have known the connection between my father, mother, and Samuels if someone didn't tell him that? And if someone did tell Greg Gamble that, who was it?

Several other questions came to mind, but were cut off by the sight of my father entering the visiting room. It had only been a few months since my last visit, but for some reason, I felt like I hadn't seen my father in years. I also noticed that my father resembled Alphonso Ribeiro, the guy that played Carlton on *The Fresh Prince of Bel-Air*. I stood up as he approached.

My father grabbed me, picked me up, and spun me around, as always. "Hey, baby girl. How are you?"

"I'm good, Dad," I replied and sat down.

"You know I can tell when something's on your mind," my father said as he sat across from me. "Talk to me. Is it the news you couldn't tell me over the phone?"

Pull yourself together, The voice inside my head said. To my father I replied, "Dad I'm good. Everything is good. I'm just tired, haven't been getting a lot of sleep lately with all the work I been doing. Now, as for the news I bring, it's good news, Dad. Jonathan Zucker called me and asked for a meeting. I went to his office and he dropped a bomb in my lap. Do you remember Maryann Settles?"

The expression on my father's face stiffened. "How could I not? Hot bitch lied on me at trial and said I killed Dontay Samuels. When someone gets on a witness stand, points you out ,and lies on you, that's some shit you never forget."

"I can only imagine. Well, the good news is, that 'hot bitch' has come forward to recant her story. She sent a three-page affidavit to Gary Kolman's office, since he was co-counsel on your case and Abe Shankel is now deceased. Gary opened the mail, the affidavit, read it, and immediately called Jon Zucker. Jon picked it up, authenticated it, and then called me. Yesterday, I went to Jon's office and read the affidavit. It's a beauty, Dad, implicating Greg Gamble. Maryann Settles says that she was coerced, paid and instructed to get on the stand in your trial and lie. According to her, she never witnessed the murder. She wasn't even there on Sheridan Road that day."

"Wait a minute." My father dropped his head and dragged both palms over it.   "She said that she was paid to lie?"

I nodded.

"That's what she says in the affidavit. That Greg Gamble paid her to get on the stand and implicate you as the person who killed Dontay Samuels. She said that she sent an innocent man to prison and that it's been eating at her soul."

"Conscience must have had a slow appetite."

"Dad, I'ma need you to focus, okay? Maryann Settles goes on to say that she was somewhere else at the time of the murder and that can be verified."

"After all these years?"

"That's what she said. The affidavit was handwritten, then typed. Both copies were signed by Maryann Settles, witnessed by her husband Christopher, and notarized by a notary."

My father's face was unreadable. "I can't believe it. Why come forward after sixteen years?"

"Beats me," I said and shrugged my shoulders. "Maybe she's going through a midlife crisis or some sort of a religious phase. Who knows? The affidavit doesn't say why she decided to come forward after all these years, just that she does. She says that… oh, it was eating at her. But she goes on to say that she'd be willing to say everything she said in the affidavit in open court, if necessary. Even if she has to face perjury charges. Jonathan Zucker believes that not only does this free you, it creates a scandal at the U.S. Attorney's office that Greg Gamble can't stand up under."

"Fuck Greg Gamble and his whole family."

"Speaking of Greg Gamble, do you know him personally?"

"Personally? What do you mean by personally? He was the prosecutor on my case."

"I mean, did you know him before you got locked up? I ask because all this shit with him seems personal."

"Personal?" my father repeated.

"Yeah, personal. And this whole Maryann Settles affidavit makes that point even more. Add that to the crazy shit he said to me at the court building. I thought that he was just messed up at me because he made his bones off of the Sean Branch case and I helped to free him."

"What crazy shit did that nigga say to you?"

"I got a client named David Battle. He's locked up——"

"I know Lil Dave. His sister Sherry, brother Big Tony, and Lil Rick grew up with me."

"Never knew that," I said and continued my spiel. "Dave's witnesses were all murdered in the last few months. Greg Gamble wants the judge to allow him to proceed to trial with just written statements from the deceased witnesses. The judge, Gary Kalfani, is a former prosecutor and has been known to be partial to 555, so I expect him to rule in Gamble's favor. If he does, David is a shoo-in for reversal on appeal, but I'm trying to stop it from going that far. We had a hearing last week to argue the merits of Greg Gamble's motion and my motion to oppose his. I left the courtroom and was confronted by Greg Gamble."

"Confronted? By Gamble? What did he say?"

"Ms. Carter, I need to have a word with you," Greg Gamble said

"Well, speak," I replied.

"I was thinking maybe a sit down at a cafe..."

"Okay, let's talk here."

"Do you really think it's smart to go toe to toe with a man like me?"

"Toe to toe? Excuse me, but are we officers of the court, or are we boxers?"

"I thought that maybe we could civilly come to some type of an agreement, but I see that you want to play hardball. So, let's play."

"Are you a closeted sports buff or something, because all of your sports cliches are a little asinine."

"Your client thought that he was doing himself a favor by having all of the witnesses against him killed. He thought that that would free him. But he's wrong. Just like your father was wrong..."

"What? His bitch ass said that?

I nodded. "His words exactly. Verbatim."

"Piece of shit faggot. I wish I could break his fuckin' neck."

"Well, you can't. Then next he said…"

"You didn't think I knew who you were? I didn't get to the top seat in the United States Attorney's office because of my good looks. I got there by doing my homework. I'm a research buff and I have the ability to memorize everything that I've ever heard or seen. When I first heard your name, I knew that it sounded familiar. But I didn't figure it out right away. When I saw you for the first time on TV before the Sean Branch retrial, it came to me. Not to mention the resemblance. It's uncanny. Although it's been sixteen years, every case I've ever prosecuted is stuck in my head. I had to go back and check my files, but sure enough, there it was. Zinfandel Carter and Michael Carter are related. The day that he got found guilty in

court, he screamed out, 'I love you, Zin!' I never forgot that. It was touching. A condemned man's love for his only daughter. Did daddy's little girl come off the porch and become a lawyer to wrestle around in the criminal justice yard with the big dogs? Then again, don't answer that. But let me tell you that behind the scenes, your father had people from the Trinidad organization try and intimidate witnesses. A few were even killed. But in any fight where there's good versus evil, good will always prevail. I found a way then to produce other witnesses and secure a conviction against your father. And I will repeat history in this same courtroom by finding a way to convict your current client. David Battle will never see the light of day again. Not as long as I am alive and breathing. And you know why? Because of you. You decided to fuck with my office. You should have stayed away from Sean Branch. And you should have stayed away from this case. But since you didn't, I have to put you humbly back in your place. And that, my dear, is in the kitchen or a hip hop video somewhere. It's personal to me now..."

"Fuck Greg Gamble. I could have been——"

I waited patiently for my father to finish his sentence, but he never did. "Dad, you could have been what? What were you gonna say just now? And is that all you can say?"

"Nothing, baby. Forget it. Don't pay that coward no mind. He's just mad because I..."

Again, an unfinished sentence.

"When Greg Gamble said that you had people from the Trinidad organization trying to intimidate witnesses and what he said about witnesses getting killed——"

"He lied. If that was the case, why were the remaining two allowed to live to testify? He was just tryna rattle your cage. And speaking of two witnesses, if Maryann Settles has recanted, they still have Thomas Turnels. What about that?"

"Good question. I'm not exactly sure how that works. You gotta ask Jon Zucker that question."

"Cool, I will. But back to your original question. Did I know Greg Gamble before I got charged with Dontay Samuel's murder?

The answer is no. Never met him until he got assigned to prosecute my case. He tried to get me to cop and tell on people. I refused."

"It makes no sense then. Why would he pay Maryann Settles to lie on you?" Zin asked.

"I don't have a clue to why he'd do that."

"So, where did he get your name from and how did he know about Mom getting killed?"

"He's a prosecutor, Zin. They dine with cops. They know everything about crimes committed."

"I get that part, but why did he theorize that you killed Dontay Samuels because he killed your wife?"

My father was starting to look very uncomfortable. "I don't know. Hey, could you get me some snacks from the vending machine? I think my sugar is getting low."

"Sure, Dad. What snacks do you want?"

"Something sweet, something salty. And chocolate. You decide."

I grabbed my change purse and walked over to the bevy of vending machines for my father. I got Skittles, Starburst, Jalapeno Cheetos, and a variety of candy bars. For myself, I got Ruffles Sour Cream and Cheddar chips. I went back to where my father was and put all the snacks on the table in between us.

"Thank you, baby girl." My father opened the Skittles and dumped several into his hand. He tossed them into his mouth a few at a time.

"I just thought about something, Dad."

"What's that, Zin?"

"If you didn't kill Dontay Samuels, then who did?"

"I don't have a clue. How am I supposed to know? I wasn't even there that night."

"You've always said that, but honestly, I just thought you were saying that because you didn't want me to think you were a cold-blooded murderer."

"No, I told you that because it was true. I didn't kill Dontay Samuels."

"So, here's my issue with that. Ever since I was nine years old, I've been told that you killed Dontay Samuels because he killed my mother. Is that true?"

"Is what true? Which part, I mean?"

"If the truth is that you didn't kill Dontay Samuels, did he really kill my mother?"

"I don't know if he did or not. I can't say."

"Did you know him, Dad?" I asked.

The look on my father's face was priceless. It was as if the Skittles he was eating were filled with shit instead of fruity nougat. "Did I know who?"

"Dontay Samuels."

"Where are all of these questions coming from, Zin? No, I didn't know Dontay Samuels."

You lying piece of shit! My inner voice screamed out. "They're coming from curiosity, Dad. Maryann Settles' affidavit opened up a can of worms, and they're crawling all over my shoes. All my life, I've lived with the narrative that this teenager named Dontay Samuels, in a senseless act of violence, beat, raped, and killed my mother. And then you searched for him, found him, and killed him to avenge my mother's death. Although you've repeatedly said that you didn't commit the murder, I always thought you were just saying that to regain your freedom. But now that it's come out that you are truly innocent and Greg Gamble paid people to lie on you at trial, now I'm left with more questions than answers. And the main questions in my head are, if you didn't kill Dontay, who did? And whether or not Dontay Samuels killed my mother. If he didn't, who did? What if there were more than one person involved in Mommy's death?"

"Zin, please, stop this right now. Stop with all the questions. The past belongs in the past. There's no sense in rehashing all of that now. Let's just concentrate on the future and getting me out of prison. How long do you think it'll take before I know whether or not that affidavit from Maryann Settles will free me?"

"I don't know, Dad, but hopefully, it won't take long. Jon Zucker should be preparing a newly discovered evidence motion as we speak. I'll call him once I leave here."

***

I left USP Canaan feeling like I'd just spent three hours in a hole. I felt like I needed another shower. There were questions in my head that I had no answers for. But there was one question that I could answer. Was my father a lying muthafucka? The answer was yes. My father looked me right in the face on several occasions and lied through his teeth. Michael Carter was guilty of all the charges against him that my heart had indicted him on. I sat in my car and did the only thing I could do. I cried.

If You Cross Me Once 2

Chapter 7
BLAST

"Your brother was always with Whistle," Chock from Valley Green said. "But Whistle had other friends that he brought through here. Doo Doo from up the Lane and the dude Miguel from Orleans Place over Northeast. That's all I can tell you, bruh."

I pulled out money from my pocket and paid Chock for the weed he sold me. "Thanks, homie, I appreciate it. If you see Whistle, tell him that Blast said to call him."

"Got you, bruh."

The sun was high in the sky and shining bright as I walked up Valley Avenue. The temperature had to be in the nineties. Tossing the mid-grade Arizona weed into the grass by the curb, I climbed back into Ren's Infiniti truck.

"Did you learn anything?" Ren asked.

"You hip to the dude Miguel from Orleans?"

"Of course. Miguel went to Hamilton with me. He getting all the money over there on that side. Why? What's up with him?"

"Nothing, yet. I just found out that Whistle hangs out with him. If I can find him, maybe he knows where I can find Whistle."

"So, you want me to go to Orleans Place to see if Miguel is there?"

I nodded. "Would you, please? I'd appreciate it."

"Anything for you, baby. Even if it means being your chauffeur."

***

There was a white Mercedes Benz S550 parked on the corner of Fourth Street. Orleans Place intersected it.

"That's Miguel's Benz. He must be outside."

Without saying a word, I hopped out of the truck and walked down Orleans Place. I had seen Miguel with Whistle and my brother on a few occasions. Didn't know him well, but I knew him. In front of a house in the middle of the block stood three dudes. The one in jeans and a tight Versace T-shirt with the half of medusa head emblem on it was Miguel. I walked up to the trio.

"Miguel, let me holla at you, slim."

Miguel looked me up and down. "Oh…you Crud's brother. I almost didn't recognize you, homie. Blast, right?"

I nodded.

"What's good, homes?" Miguel asked as he stepped away from his men.

"I'm tryna find Whistle, bruh. Can you direct my path?"

"I can definitely do that if you looking for Whistle. By now his body should be at the city morgue over by D.C. General. Whistle got wiped down last night in a house on Third Street. Somebody wiped him and another nigga down and set the house on fire. Somebody put the fire out or some shit so he didn't get burned too bad. His mother called me and told me. The cops got in touch with her to ID the body. She called me after she confirmed that it was him. She told me that there was another body in that house, too."

"That was my brother, bruh. The other nigga was my brother."

"Who, Crud?"

I nodded my head.

"Damn, slim, I didn't know that. But homes, I gotta keep it a band with you. I ain't surprised to hear that Whistle and Crud got wiped down like that. Both of them knew that niggas had money on their heads. I know that because we talked about it."

"Y'all talked about it?" I repeated. "My brother talked to you about somebody putting a hit out on him?"

"Yeah. Crud thought that shit was funny. He didn't believe that he could get lit. Whistle was more afraid though. He was always paranoid. You need to go around Park Chester or up the Lane and holla at Doo Doo."

"Do you know who put the money on my brother's head?"

"I can't say for sure who put up the money but I know what the money was put up about."

"Is that right?"

"Yeah. Two years ago, me, Crud, Whistle, and Doo Doo went on a move to get a nigga who Whistle said had over a hundred pounds of OG and a rack of money in his house. The move went bad when the nigga we had trapped off got away from us. Crud had taken the nigga's car and went to different ATM machines to withdraw money from the dude's debit cards. On the way back to the spot, Crud got bagged in the car."

"I remember that. He went in on an armed robbery beef."

"Armed robbery, kidnapping, burglary, and assault beef. While Crud was over the jail, he folded under pressure and jumped on Lacy and Buck and n'em case."

"Lacy and Buck?"

"Yeah, some good men from MLK Avenue went in on a conspiracy case. The ATF said they were trappin' out of a barbershop. Buckeyfields, Lacy, Calvin, Foots, Dee, one of the Venable brothers, and a dude named Lonnell. Crud was on the block with Buck and Lacy. He knew them through Whistle. They were fuckin' with Crud thinking he was solid. Talkin' about their case to him. They found out that Crud had snitched on a dude named Larry Bing back in the day. Buck confronted Crud. Crud checked into P.C. and contacted the prosecutor on Lacy n'em case. It was that wild nigga Greg Gamble. He told Gamble and the ATF that he'd being buying heroin from them niggas in the barbershop for years. They went to trial last year and Crud got on the stand against them. He cooked them niggas for two straight days. Then he told on Whistle about some shit. Whistle got locked up and told on them barbershop dudes, too. He didn't take the stand, but he made statements. Both of them got out last year, as you know. Niggas been talkin' about that shit since. Everybody knew about it. That's why Whistle and Crud been on all bullshit out here. Someone on that case put up the money I heard. Who, I don't know."

"That's what's up, bruh. I never knew anything about any of that. I heard everything you just said, and I gotta ask you this. You just said that you and my brother talked about the money being put on his head. Him and Whistle. Did they know why the money was put on their heads?"

Miguel nodded. "They knew. I told you Crud didn't give a fuck and Whistle was 'noid about it."

"And you knew then why the money was on their heads?"

"You mean did I know at the time we talked about it that Crud and Whistle was 'hot'? Yeah, I knew it. Everybody knew it."

"And you continued to fuck with them knowing they were rats?"

Miguel shrugged his shoulders. "I did. They didn't tell on me."

Smiling, I said, "Typical."

"What does that mean, slim? Typical? What's typical?"

"You, slim. Typical thug nigga. Preach the code, but don't live by it."

"Say what you want, slim, but I live by it. Your hot-ass brother didn't live by it. Him or Whistle. That's why niggas knocked them off like that."

"My hot-ass brother, huh? You knew he was hot and still hung with him, so what does that make you, slim?"

Miguel laughed and then frowned. "I'ma dismiss your disrespect as an emotional blunder given the fact that you're messed up about your brother. But I advise you not to ever play with me like that again. Like you calling me 'hot' because I didn't ostracize Whistle and Crud. If you do that again, your mother gon' be burying two sons instead of one. You feel me?"

As if they had mental telepathy and sensed that things were going bad between me and Miguel, the two dudes on the porch walked up beside Miguel.

"What's up, bruh? You good?" one dude said, lifting his shirt to reveal a big-ass chrome handgun.

"Yeah, homie," the other dude with dreads said, "you good?"

Miguel eyed both of his men. "I'm good, slim. This nigga was just leaving. Go ahead and bounce, slim, before I change my mind, and don't be good."

I raise my hands in a mock sign of surrender. "Whoa! I don't want no smoke with y'all. I'm gone." I turned around expecting to be shot, but I wasn't.

It took me ten minutes to get back to Ren's Infiniti truck. I climbed into the passenger seat with a look of death in my eyes.

"What happened?" Ren asked. "What did Miguel say?"

"He told me some shit about my brother that I didn't know. Then he threatened me."

"He threatened you? Threatened you for what?"

"Because he could, and because he don't know me very well."

Ren smiled a mischievous smile. "Naw, he don't know us very well. What do you wanna do about it?"

"It's three of them out there, and at least one of them is strapped."

"I got you, baby." Ren reached under her seat. "Let me handle this for you. They will never know what hit them." Ren tucked her gun and hopped out of the truck.

I leaned back in my seat and thought about everything Miguel said about my brother. I couldn't believe that he was accusing Crud of being a rat.

Minutes later, my train of thought was broken by the sound of gunshots. I got out of the truck and climbed into the driver's seat. I started the truck. A few minutes later, Ren got into the passenger seat.

***
Later, at Carolina Kitchen restaurant...

Ren came out of the bathroom dressed completely different. She'd even changed her hairstyle. I was still in line when she walked up. We embraced and kissed.

"I thought that you said that killing makes you horny?" I asked Ren.

She smiled, hugged me tighter, and replied, "In this particular case, it's made me hungry."

"Well, what would you like to eat?"

"I'ma get the crab cakes, some fried fish, the mac and cheese, and the fried cabbage. Some potato salad on the side, and for dessert, the banana pudding."

"Gotdamn, baby! You ain't bullshittin' when you say you hungry, huh?"

"I think it's the weed, boo. Or I might be pregnant."

"That wouldn't be bad at all. A life taken, a life given," I told Ren.

When the woman behind the counter asked for our orders, I gave her both mine and Ren's.

Ren leaned into me and kissed me. "After I take care of hungry, I gotta satisfy my horny. You with that, bae?"

"You already know."

***

"Did you catch the news?" I asked Bionca.

"Wait, hold on a minute," Bionca replied. "Let me check on Mommy right quick."

Ren sat beside me on the couch, watching a movie on Netflix, her head laid on my shoulder.

"Hello, Brion?"

"I'm here, sis. I asked you, did you catch the news?"

"Naw, should I have?"

"Doesn't matter. There were three dudes hit on Orleans Place earlier today. Two dead, one at Howard fighting for his life." I went on to tell Bionca everything that Miguel told me about Crud. "Did you know he did that?"

"Naw. I never knew that, but regardless of what was said, it's a rock of niggas out here who ain't living by the code of silence. And they still alive. Why the fuck was my brother so special that niggas wanted him dead because he told? If he told. That shit ain't true just because Miguel said it. Even if it is true, he was still our rat, and like I keep saying, nobody had the right to kill him like that. You gotta find Doo Doo and see what he has to say. Find out who put the money up on Crud's head. I wanna know that and I wanna know who killed him. And before my mother buries her son, I want them all to be dead."

"How the fuck I'ma kill niggas that's in jail if I find out that the dudes who Crud told on is the ones who put the money on his head?"

"Ain't nobody untouchable, brother. Them niggas got families, don't they?"

Anthony Fields

If You Cross Me Once 2

Chapter 8
MICHAL CARTER
United States Pen
Canaan

The prison rec yard was enormous, but divided into three different yards. A metal fence surrounded the yard as a whole, but it also ran through the yards to separate the three yards into one. One yard had the soccer field and asphalt track around it. The middle yard was the basketball court yard. And the other yard at the end of the walk was the softball field yard. Having been in the Feds for years, I understood that sectioning off the yards was a tactical design. With the yard separated in three, that limited the number of prisoners on any one yard at one time, thereby making it easier to respond and quell any violence or riots that broke out. Me and my partner, Kenny Simmons, walked the track around the soccer field.

"One of the witnesses in my case recanted. Signed an affidavit saying that my prosecutor at the time, Greg Gamble, paid her to lie on me."

Kenny's attention was elsewhere. His eyes were focused on something across the yard. Just as I was about to repeat myself, he said, "That's good news, soldier. But an affidavit only gets you an evidentiary hearing because it's newly discovered evidence. Is the judge in case still alive?"

"Naw. Judge Victor Wise died a couple years ago."

"So, that means that your hearing will be in front of a different judge, one with a fresh set of ears to hear new evidence about your cae. That's good thing."

"It is, but homie, the nigga Greg Gamble is the U.S. Attorney now. That nigga ain't gon let me get away like that. We got a lot of bad blood between us. My daughter even picked up on it. She asked me did I have a personal beef with that nigga Gamble and I lied to her. Told her no."

"She don't know y'all history, huh?" Kenny asked, then looked across the yard. "Look over there, soldier. See all them dudes huddled up by the tables over there?"

"Yeah, I see 'em. Look like the Muslims and South niggas."

"That's who it is. The South dude, Ratchet, from New Orleans went to the SHU and took his shahada. Now he is Saleem Shahid or something like that. He got out the SHU yesterday and told the South dudes that he on Muslim time now. His homies are saying that he can't flip cars like that. Deebo from Carolina got the South car on the blue side. He saying that Ratchet gotta go to another yard and be Muslim. He saying Ratchet can't stay here and that he gotta go. The Imam on the red side sent word to Mike P——"

"That's Mustafa, right?"

"Yeah. He sent word to Mustafa and told him to stand with the new convert. He says that Ratchet is under the Shahada and the Muslim protection so he ain't gotta go nowhere. That's what they politicking about right now. It looks like it ain't going to good over there. I can read the body language. You strapped?"

I thought about the hard, sharpened fiberglass knife I had cheeked and replied, "I got the floater on me. Why?"

"Because when shit gets hectic, dudes don't be knowing who is who. I got that steel on me. I'ma burn somebody's ass up if shit comes this way. What was you saying before…oh, you was talking about Greg Gamble. You got Sean Branch to kill his peoples, right?" Kenny asked.

"Yeah. His brother owed me for some coke and refused to pay the bill. Thought he was untouchable. I had to show him that he wasn't."

"How did you come to meet that guy and how does Greg Gamble know it was you who got his brother hit?"

"I'm still tryna figure out how he knew that. Haven't got a clue after all these years. But it's crazy how shit happens. I met this chick at the Masonic temple one night. We started fuckin'. She introduced me to her brother. I wasn't plugged in at that time. Cindy - that's the chick I was fuckin' - put me on with her brother. Lonnell Gamble was getting to it back then. He was connected to Carlos Cardoza Junior. I copped coke from him until Cardoza Junior got killed. Niggas found out he was a federal informant the whole time."

"Who, Lonnell Gamble or Carlos Cardoza Junior?"

If You Cross Me Once 2

"Carlos Cardoza Junior. That's why he got smashed on Hanover."

"Heard about that . Not the informant part, but him getting killed. I know the father, Carlos Senior."

"After Carlos Junior got wiped down, Lonnell started fuckin with Frey. But then Frey got wiped down too. So, he was on his knuckles for a minute. I got plugged into a migo nigga named Victor Martinez. He was fucking with Carlos Trinidad."

"The Spanish kingpin nigga?"

"Yeah. Make a long story short, the nigga Vic was fucked up. Trinidad found out and offered me the hit. I killed Vic and started coping bricks straight from Trinidad. Cindy found out and put Lonnell on my line. I started fronting him bricks. Everything was cool, until he fucked the money up one time. I let that go. Fronted him two more bricks to get right and the nigga refused to pay me. Said the work was stepped on. That was bullshit. Everything I got from Trinidad was fishscale and I never touched it. Always sold it as is. It was the best coke in the city. I tried to talk to Lonnell, but he got gangsta with me. Pissed me off. I was gon' crush him, but Ameen wanted him. After doing my homework, we saw that it was gon' be hard to get to him. We found out that he had a new connect and was feeding a rack of killers. They stayed around him at all times. That's when Ameen decided to put the young boy on him."

"Sean Branch?"

I nodded.

"Sean was like fourteen or fifteen then. Looked like he was ten or eleven. He got up on Lonnell with no problem and nailed his ass to the ground. But I forgot to mention that on a couple of occasions when I met up with Lonnell Gamble, he had his brother Greg with him. I never knew who was older or younger, just that the brother Greg was in Law school. After Lonnell got killed …"

"ALL INMATES ON THE YARD GET DOWN ON THE GROUND OR YOU WILL BE SHOT!" the compound loudspeakers belted out. Then an explosion rocked the ground. "ALL INMATES ON THE YARD GET DOWN ON THE GROUND OR YOU WILL BE SHOT!"

Anthony Fields

I got on the ground beside Kenny. I looked over by the tables. The Muslims and the South dudes were getting it in in an all-out brawl. Dudes were getting chased and stabbed on both sides. I saw Kenny pull the knife he had on him. I did the same. But responding staff was so deep, so fast, that the brawl was over quick. I tossed the floater into the high grass near the Bocce court. Kenny threw his knife over by the fence. In seconds, ten COs were on us.

"See you when we come off lockdown, soldier," Kenny said before being led away to his unit.

"Yeah, this one might be awhile," I replied to myself.

"What unit you in?!" One of the CO's asked me.

"I'm in E-1."

***

"How long you think this lockdown gon' last, homie?"

My celly Henry Lil Man James was a little burnt out after being locked down in ADX for almost thirteen years. He climbed on the top bunk and laid down.

"Depends on whether or not any of them niggas die. Since it was two different cars, they gotta investigate and all that. Make sure the Muslim's and the South gon agree to not go at it again. They probably gon' ship a rack of niggas out and then let us up. Depends."

The next thing I heard was Lil Man snoring.

***

"Take your shirt off and spin around for me, guy," the redneck CO said

I complied with his every command. I knew the routine by heart. I put my hands out and let him see my hands on both sides.

"A'ight. Now, your celly."

After the upper body check, I laid down and thought about the visit with Zin. The questions she asked me wouldn't leave my mind.

If You Cross Me Once 2

I thought about Cindy Gamble. I thought about Lonnell Gamble. I thought the past history that had me linked to the Gamble family.

"Speaking of Greg Gamble, do you know him personally?"

"Personally? What do you mean by personally? He was the prosecutor on my case."

"I mean, did you know him before you got locked up? I ask because all this shit with him seems personal."

I thought about how I had looked Zin in the face and told her that I didn't know Greg Gamble before getting locked up for Dontay's murder and how nothing between us was personal. But then I thought about what Greg Gamble had told Zin …

"Your client thought that he was doing himself a favor by having all the witnesses against him killed. He thought that would free him, but he was wrong. Just like your father was wrong…"

And the reality of it was that everything between Greg Gamble and me was personal.

Anthony Fields

Chapter 9
MICHAEL CARTER
THE PAST
1995
Homicide Division
Pennsylvania Avenue and Branch

The white paper jumpsuit I was dressed in was starting to tear in all the wrong places. I could feel the air from the tiny room's air conditioner creeping up my back and seeping into my butt crack.

"We already know why you killed him, Mike. Don't mind if I call you Mike, do you?" the white Tom Cruise-looking detective asked. I didn't respond. "Not talking, huh? Okay, so I'ma assume that you don't have a problem with me calling you Mike. The streets call you Mike, right? Mike Carter, right?"

No response.

The black detective in the room was tall. Had to be at least 6'4" and built like an offensive lineman on any NFL team. His Alabama Crimson Tide sweatshirt was a little too snug for his frame. While the white detective was seated across from me, the black one leaned on the wall. He walked up close to me.

"Chase, let me try. Mr. Carter, my name is Detective Jones. Believe it or not, we're trying to help you. Help you help yourself, if that makes any sense to you. We got two tips on the hotline. One that you killed Dontay Samuels and two, the murder weapon could be found in an apartment you rent. The gun was found, but it hasn't been confirmed as the actual murder weapon. But it will be eventually, if it is, in fact, the gun that killed Dontay Samuels. If you didn't kill Dontay Samuels and you know who did——"

"I don't know shit and I didn't kill anybody," I said, emotionally drained.

"You lying piece of shit. You going down."

"Hey, Chase, be cool, partner. Let me talk to Mr. Carter."

"Naw, A.J., fuck him!" White Detective exploded. "We're trying to fucking help the guy, and he's giving us his fuckin' ass to kiss!"

Anthony Fields

Classic good cop/bad cop antics didn't fool me. My feathers were unrufflable. I smiled at their tactics.

"Mr. Carter…listen, it's Mike, right? Listen to me. My partner is a little stressed out. But I'm calm. You're calm. Here's the thing. You're about to do hard time for a murder that I don't think you committed. You don't have to do any time if you cooperate with us. Dontay Jamal Samuels was a deviant, incorrigible piece of shit. The stinkiest piece of the turd either at the tip or the end. His juvenile rap sheet is as long as this table right here. His name has come up several times recently in unsolved murders. Trust me when I say that nobody's gonna miss him. Nobody in law enforcement is upset over his death. Somebody did the world a favor by killing him. I need you to talk to me, Mike. If not about this case, about some other cases. Throw us a bone or two and we'll get you out of this mess. I promise you that. You're from the Sheridan Terrace area. Tell us who killed Juan 'Zip' Lyles and Tee Tinch. Who killed Eric Miles? Who killed Big Head Ronnie and Bernadette on Sheridan Road by the phone booths? Tell us who killed Skeeter and Terrance. Who killed Cat Eye Lucky and Poppa Two? Who killed Black Boochie and Big Lip Stink? You're a major player in the area, Mike. We know who you are. Give us something on these cold cases and I promise you, you'll walk right out that door. So, tell me, Mike, do you wanna go home or go to prison?"

"You got the wrong guy. On the murder and on the rat tip. I ain't got nothing else to say. I need a lawyer."

White Detective stood up and laughed. "Okay, Mike, have it your way. Believe it or not, I can respect that. Keep quiet. All the quiet ones are still at Lorton looking stupid on the rec yard. Glad you wanna join them. C'mon, A.J., this interview is over. Your transport will be here shortly."

***
Three weeks later…

Twenty-seven prisoners, including myself, were shuffled off the court bus, handcuffed to a belly chain and shackled at the feet. Upstairs, we were headed to a bevy of different holding cages.

As the cuffs were being removed, one U.S. Marshall said, "Wait a minute, who's Carter? Michael Carter?"

"I'm right here," I called out.

"Step this way. You're going somewhere else," the marshall told me.

I was beyond confused. "Fuck I'm going at?"

"Shut the fuck up and come with me."

Already knowing that the U.S. Marshal's service was notorious for giving out grade-A ass whippings at the court building, I did exactly as I was told. I was ushered out of the building into a waiting van. The drive down the street was short. I was pulled out of the van and herded through a labyrinth of hallways until we reached a small conference room.

"Sit down in one of the chairs at the table," the marshal demanded. Then he left the room.

"Where the fuck am I?" I asked myself.

My question was answered ten minutes later when a beautiful, blond-haired, white woman walked into the room. "Michael Carter, hello. My name is Susan Rosenthal and I'm an assistant U.S. Attorney here at the Triple Nickel."

"Triple Nickel?"

"Yeah, we who work here call this building The Triple Nickel because of its address, 555 Fourth Street. I assume this is your first time at the United States Attorney's Office. Can I get you something to eat? Drink?"

"Naw, I'm good. But you can tell me why I'm here."

"I've heard so much about you that I wanted to meet you. But you're here to see one of my colleagues. He'll be in to see you shortly. He's in a meeting that's running a little late. So, for a little while, you're stuck with me. Thought maybe you'd want to talk. I mean, you didn't want to talk when you were arrested three weeks ago, but maybe after spending time at the D.C. jail, you might've changed your mind."

"I haven't," I replied, curtly.

"Well, that's too bad——" the white woman said, but stopped mid-sentence when the door to the conference room opened and in walked a man that I hadn't seen in years.

The man still looked exactly the same. I recognized him instantly.

"Susan, you can leave now. Thanks for coming down here, but I need to have a few private words with Mr. Carter, if you don't mind."

Susan Rosenthal looked at Greg Gamble, then at me. She stood and left the room without a backward glance, closing the door behind her.

"I ain't got shit to say to you, Mr. Prosecutor," I told Greg Gamble.

"Who said anything about you talking? Not me. I didn't bring you here to talk. Nothing you could possibly say would interest me. I brought you here to listen," Greg Gamble hissed as walked up to within a foot of where I sat handcuffed and shackled. "It's been awhile, but I hope you didn't think that I forgot about you. How could I? I know that it was you who had my brother killed in that salon." Greg Gamble clapped his hands together suddenly. "Sending a teenager into the salon dressed like a school kid was a stroke of genius. Bravo! Nobody expected the kid to kill my brother. I also know that your partner, Ameen Bashir, was involved. He picked the teen up in a red BMW after the murder. Then, to add insult to injury, you had the audacity to come to my brother's funeral and hug my sister. You watched my family grieve, all the while knowing that you were the one who put my brother in the casket up there.

"Then a few years later, when my sister Cindy was gunned down on Wade Road, people said that Cindy had set up some out-of-town drug dealers and her death was retaliation for that. Cindy was about that life and everybody accepted the rumors about her death because the end result fit the narrative. Wool was pulled over everyone's eyes but mine. When I learned that the person who killed Cindy resembled a young child, I knew the person who ordered her death was you. After Lonnell's murder, you had her killed. Again,

If You Cross Me Once 2

bravo!" Greg Gamble clapped again. "Job well done. You fooled everybody but me. It's been a long time coming, but I finally have you right where I want you. And I bet you're wondering what I mean by that, right? Well, let me tell you. I know that you killed Ameen Bashir. I know that Ameen's son works *and kills* for you. I know that Dontay Samuels killed for you. I know that you didn't kill him. Quran Bashir, Ameen's oldest son, killed Dontay. What I don't know is why. I know that your wife Patricia Carter was killed a month and a half ago. Found beaten, raped, and strangled I wanna say that you either killed her or had her killed. I'm not sure which, but you were involved in her death. I can feel it. She was your wife, so fuck her. Let's get back to Dontay Samuels, the seventeen-year-old that you are charged with killing. I have witnesses who are going to put you at the scene firing a gun——"

"You can't fucking do that!" I shouted.

Greg Gamble smiled. "I can and I will. The gun that was taken out of the apartment you leased. It's not the murder weapon, but by the time I'm finished with you, it will be. The anonymous caller that called and gave authorities the tips about you and the gun…that was ME. I'm gonna play that call at trial for the jury. Wait, did I get too far ahead of myself? I mentioned a trial, because there will be a trial. I am not offering you any plea offers whatsoever. So, at trial, I'm going to convince twelve jurors that you killed Dontay Samuels. Why? Because he killed and raped your wife. Then I'm going to convince the judge at your sentencing to give you the maximum amount of time allowed. Life in prison. End of story."

Greg Gamble turned to leave. Then he stopped and turned back to face me. "And two more things, Mike. I sent Sean Branch to prison for life a couple years ago. Not because he killed Raymond Watson. I know that he didn't do that. You did. I sent him to prison for life because I knew that it was him who killed my brother in the salon. And don't fret. Quran Bashir will be joining you as soon as he's done enough to be tried as an adult for murders that I will be sure he'll commit. Or ones that I will put on him. Take care, Mike. I'll see you at trial."

"Hey, Gamble. One question. Why Quran? Why are you after him?"

"You know the answer to that question, Mike. Quran Bashir killed my sister Cindy."

Chapter 10
MICHAEL CARTER
THE PRESENT

Coming clean to Zin about my history with Greg Gamble wasn't an option. Opening that can of worms wasn't worth the fish that the bait would catch. Everything that Greg Gamble had said to me in that room over sixteen years ago had come to pass. Just as he said it would. I thought about everything that he said to me. After all these years, I still couldn't figure out how Greg Gamble knew all the stuff he knew. The part about me ordering the death of his brother was pure conjecture, but easily concluded. But how had he known that it was Sean Branch who had killed his brother? How did he know that Ameen was the one who had picked up Sean after the murder? How had he learned about the Raymond Watson murder and that I was the one who killed Raymond? I know why he prosecuted Sean for Raymond's murder, but why not just come after me for it? How in the hell had he known about Quran killing Dontay? How had he figured out that it was Quran who killed his sister Cindy? No matter how many times I asked myself these questions, no answers ever came to me.

I thought about Maryann Settles and the three-page affidavit that Jon Zucker had from her. Her allegations of being paid to lie on me by Greg Gamble had to mean something to the courts. But would it be enough to overturn my conviction? Would a new judge be objective and partial to my newly-discovered evidence? And what about Thomas Turner, the second witness against me? He'd also been paid to lie on me. After taking the stand against me, the men had disappeared into thin air. Would he have to resurface to give perjured testimony once again? If he did, I promised myself that Thomas Turner would not escape death a second time. I'd pay the highest price for his life. I didn't care who had to be sacrificed to bring about his demise. Quran, Jihad, and Sean would hunt for the man when I put the money on his head. And I was confident that they'd find and kill Thomas Turner.

Anthony Fields

Then suddenly, a different thought hit me. Why hadn't I heard anything from Sean Branch? He had my number. Quran told me that he'd given it to him when he first got released from jail. Having been home for three weeks already and not contacting me was puzzling. Should I take his reticence as a sign of discord? Although we both have been incarcerated in the Bureau of Prisons for years, our paths never crossed. He had never reached out to me and neither had I reached out to him. Although I knew that Sean felt some kind of way about being sentenced to life for a murder I committed, it wasn't my fault, and he knew that. I wasn't the one who'd built the case against him. Then another thought hit. I had the opportunity to put Quran on Reese and didn't. Maybe that was Sean's reason for not contacting me. It had to be. Or maybe I was just overthinking things. Maybe Sean was just more focused on the debts he was settling.

Having a cell phone in prison had its advantages. It allowed me to be plugged into the streets the way most prisoners could not be. It allowed me to Google newspaper articles and to tune in and watch the local news in D.C. Therefore, I knew all about the homicidal rampage that Sean was on. Detectives in D.C. didn't know who killed Maurice "Reese" Payne in a basement of a house on Longfellow Street, but I did. Raquel Dunn had been pulled out of the Potomac River dismembered. Raquel Dunn was Sean's daughter's mother. Why he killed her, I didn't know. But the fact that Sean killed her, I did know. Three other men in the city were found dead: Leon Clea, Tracy Kay, and Eric Kay. The latter two were brothers. All three were rats. All connected to Sean. All dead. Then there was Rick and Frank Bailey, two men that the local news reported as brothers, having been found dead. But in all actuality, Rick and Frank were cousins. The two men had been arrested for the murder of Sean's best friend, Stretch, in 2003. They had two hung juries before being released on a plea deal with time served. A jury couldn't find both men guilty, but Sean Branch did. He'd quickly found both men and killed them. I made a mental note to get Sean's number from Quran and call him. It was time that we talked.

If You Cross Me Once 2

Pushing Sean from my head, I sat up on the bunk. I stared at the two pictures that were taped to my locker. Zin and Patricia, my daughter and my wife. My cheating wife. The one thing I had always prided myself on back in the day was the fact that I never cheated on my wife. Never. And I had too many opportunities to do it. But I never did. Never wanted to. To me, Patricia Carter was all the woman I needed. She was my everything. I loved her with all my heart and soul. Until she betrayed me. Broke my heart into pieces. I thought about what Zin asked me...

"...if you didn't kill Dontay, who did? Did Dontay Samuel really kill my mother? And if he didn't, who did?"

There were things that I could never tell Zin. Secrets that had to always remain secrets. I laid back on the bunk and let myself be transported back to 1995...

THE PAST

"I can't take this anymore, Mike," Patricia said as she whisked into the room.

I looked up from the money counting machine on the table into the face of my wife. I could see the tears in her eyes. "You can't take what anymore?"

"This," my wife answered, sweeping her arm across her body. "This is all you care about. You walk around here and act like you don't see me. You don't talk to me. You don't touch me. I feel like I'm living with a stranger."

"Do you really want to do this right now? Are you serious?"

With a wounded look on her face, Patricia replied, "Yes, I'm serious, and why wouldn't I want to do this right now? I need to know what the fuck is going on with you."

"What's going on with me? What's going on with me? You're about to take the dirt off an already-buried corpse. Do you really want to know what's going on with me?"

"You keep answering my questions with more questions. And what do you mean by I'm taking dirt off an already-buried corpse? Fuck does that mean? I'm sick of wondering what's on your mind.

You act like you don't love me anymore. Hell, I don't even think you like me anymore. What is it that I did to you to make you act so distant? Huh? Why am I even still here? Just to be a mother to Zin? Because if that's why I'm here, I can be a mother to her from somewhere else."

"My daughter will never live apart from me! Ever!"

"Fine. Have it your way. But it's time for me to go. It's obvious that you don't want me here. You've completely shut me out. You're turned into a person that I don't know, and I don't even know why. And it ain't like this just started. You've been this way for years. You disrespect me in front of people. There's no affection between us. No love. I've been living like this for too long, Mike. I can't live like this anymore. I can't. You can raise Zin if you want to, but I'm leaving you. I have to get away from here. From you."

"You want to get away from me?" I said and laughed. "You say that you want to leave here. Leave me. Patricia, you already left me. You left me four years ago when you decided that it was a good idea to betray me. Betray our vows. Betray our marriage."

"Betray our vows? Our marriage? How did I——"

I stood up and faced my wife. "C'mon, Pat, don't look so confused. You know exactly that I'm talking about. You know me. You know who I am, what I do. You know all about the animal that lives inside me, but yet, you did it anyway."

"I did what? What did I do? How did I betray you? Us?"

"By fucking Ameen Bashir behind my back."

Patricia's entire facial expression changed to one of defeat. She dropped her head. "You were here that night. You saw us, didn't you?"

I nodded my head as tears filled my eyes. "My trip with Carlos Trinidad ended earlier than expected. I flew home the same day I left."

"You've known about this for years, and yet you said nothing."

"My actions spoke louder than words."

"But, why? Why didn't you say anything?"

"I don't know. I asked myself that question every day. Maybe I didn't want to talk about it. Talking about it would have made it real. And believe me, I wanted to act like it wasn't. Act like it never happened. Maybe it was because of Zin."

"So, why bring it up now?"

"Because you made me say it. You started this, Pat. Not me. I was sitting here counting money when you walked in with this 'I can't take it no more' shit. Did you think I was just gonna let you talk and not say shit? Did you think I was gonna just let you leave here and walk off into the sunset without speaking my piece? If you thought that, you thought wrong. Besides all that, you asked me what did you do and I told you."

"I always suspected that you were here that night. I told Ameen that you were here, that you saw us. But he convinced me that I was just being paranoid. That I had just heard a bump in the night. But then when Ameen was killed a few days later, I knew. I wasn't sure, but I believed I knew."

"You believed that you knew what, Patricia?"

"You already know. You just want me to say it, though."

"Say it, Pat. Tell me what you know."

"I knew that it was you who killed Ameen. You went to his house and killed him. I felt it."

"You were right, then, Pat. Because I did kill him. I had to."

"You had to? You killed Ameen because you had to? Why did you have to?"

"Because he betrayed me. He crossed me. And if someone crosses you once, they'll cross you twice. Carlos Trinidad told me that the day I witnessed him execute a man's entire family, all because that man had crossed him once. Then I remembered that I had heard that saying before. Ameen Bashir had told me the same thing on a couple occasions. After I caught the two of you together, I couldn't get that out of my head. So, I talked to Carlos Trinidad. Do you know what I found out? I found out that Ameen had already known Carlos before I did. That he had taken some hits for Carlos before. I found out that it was Ameen who suggested to Carlos that I be hooked up with Victoriano Martinez to buy cocaine from him. One day, I was summoned to meet with Carlos Trinidad himself. I took Ameen with me. And all the while, Ameen never told me that he already knew Carlos. He made me believe that he was meeting the man for the first time that day. I couldn't understand why Ameen would do that. I learned from Carlos that once it had become known that Victoriano Martinez had been working with the Feds, Ameen told Carlos to send me to kill Victoriano. After I did that, I dealt with Carlos directly. That was Ameen's plan. When Carlos told Ameen that he was going to New York to kill Victoriano's family, Ameen told Carlos to take me with him so that I could witness Carlos's brand of street justice firsthand. And Carlos agreed. For me to witness retribution and ruthlessness on that level, it would make me never cross Carlos. At least that's why Carlos thought Ameen was telling him to take me to New York. But then I learned different. Ameen orchestrated my absence to be able to get to you. He just never thought I'd return so soon. After the night I caught the two of you in bed, I entertained the thought of letting Ameen live. But after talking to Carlos Trinidad, I was sure that Ameen had to die. By doing everything I just said, Ameen crossed me. I couldn't give him the chance to cross me again."

"What about me, Mike?" Patricia asked.

"What about you?" I replied

"I crossed you, too, didn't I? Ameen didn't rape me."

"Ameen didn't rape you. You got a point there, Pat. And yes, you did cross me. But before I tell you why you are still alive, let me ask you something. Something that I've asked myself for years. By Ameen orchestrating the events to get rid of me for a few days, he had to have known that you'd accept his advances. Ameen was a smart and calculated guy. He wouldn't have gone through the trouble of getting rid of me unless he was 100 percent sure that he would get you into bed. How could Ameen be sure of that fact?"

My wife looked at me and her eyes told the story. Even though they were filled with tears, I could still read them. She turned away from me and didn't say a word. I had already answered the question in my mind, but didn't want to come to grips with it. The answer to my question was in her reaction to it.

"Ameen knew the two of you would be in bed because it was planned beforehand. By either him alone or the two of you. And if that's true, then that means that it wasn't the first time that the two of you had been intimate, was it?"

Patricia wiped at the tears in her eyes, but remained quiet, never even denied it. My already broken heart shattered to pieces.

"Why, Pat? At least be woman enough to tell me why. Why wasn't I enough for you? What did I do wrong? I gave you the world. You had a good life. I gave you time, affection, all my love. I gave you a beautiful child. Why wasn't it enough? Why wasn't I enough?"

Patricia looked up at me, her eyes overflowing with tears, but still she said nothing. She walked over to the bar and fixed herself a drink. I had never seen my wife drink liquor. She drowned the contents of the glass in two swallows. Then she said, "My betrayal wasn't about you. It was never about you. Or about us. It was about me and one lie. One lie that birthed many."

"One lie?" I repeated. "What one lie?"

"Ameen Bashir."

I was completely lost and the look on my face reflected that. "Ameen?"

Patricia nodded. "Ameen Bashir has always been my lie. When you and I met——"

"At the red brick carryout on MLK Avenue. How can I forget that day?"

"You and Ameen were together that day. Do you remember that?"

"I remember that."

"I was fourteen and you were sixteen years old. I had heard a lot about you in the neighborhood. You were a young hustler that all the girls wanted. I was enamored by you because you wanted me. Although Ameen was there, for a moment, all I saw was you. When I heard you tell Ameen that I was the girl that you would marry one day, our lie was created that day. One of us should have said something that day, but neither of us did. Neither of us told you that Ameen and I had already met. Well, more than met. Ameen Bashir was the boy who'd I given myself to. I had never had sex with anyone else but him. He was the one who took my virginity.

83

He was messing with the girl next door to me in apartment 201, Martina. He would leave her and come to my house. By the time I met you, Ameen and I had been sleeping together for almost two years. Why he didn't tell you that the day we met confused me. I felt as if I wasn't good enough for him to claim. I was crying. I was smitten by you. I never said a word, either. I thought that by being with you, things between Ameen and me were over. But they weren't. He continued to pursue me and I always gave in. Even after I realized that I loved you. When we got married, I convinced myself that it was over for sure between me and Ameen. But again I was wrong. My desire for him never stopped. I couldn't resist him…"

"Is Zin my daughter, Patricia?"

"Yes, I think so. Her eyes are hazel… like yours."

"Her eyes? How do you——"

"When Ameen got married, I promised myself that I would never let him touch me again. Then his wife had their baby. A boy. He had these eyes. The grey eyes. I continued to be with Ameen whenever the chance permitted. Then I got pregnant. I remember not wanting to tell you about the pregnancy at first. But I had to. I almost lost the baby because of worry and fear. I hid my concerns from you. I prayed to God that the baby was yours. But I feared that the color of our daughter's eyes would reveal my secret. When Zin was born, the first thing I wanted to see were her eyes. They were brown. So, I knew that Zin was yours. She has your eyes. I thought that that scare would be enough to finally make me break things off with Ameen. But it didn't. I couldn't resist him…"

An uncontrollable rage took over me as I crossed the room. I smacked Patricia and she flew into the couch. Then I was on her. Knees, hands, fists, and feet.

"Michael, please! Stop! Michael!"

Even her cries and pleas for me to stop enraged me. Her blood enraged me. Like a shark in the water, I pounced. I ripped all of Patricia's clothes from her body. Then I laid her on the couch and ravished her. I penetrated every crevice on her body until I had satisfied myself completely. Patricia's cries fell on deaf ears. I forced

If You Cross Me Once 2

my dick into her mouth until she gagged and threw up. I wiped myself off and made her deep throat me. All I could see was Ameen with her in every way. In the end, I wrapped my hands around my wife's neck and squeezed. My tears fell onto her face as she struggled to breathe. She tried to find air, but there was none to be had. My hands made sure of that. Once her struggling beneath me stopped, I kept squeezing. And kept squeezing.

Anthony Fields

If You Cross Me Once 2

Chapter 11
MICHAEL CARTER
THE PAST 1995

I stood over Patricia's lifeless body and didn't regret a thing. Her last words filled my head and wouldn't leave. She and Ameen had been fucking the entire time that we'd been together. I thought about all the kisses we'd shared, all the times I had eaten her pussy. I was sickened by the thought of Ameen's cum being inside her mouth, inside her pussy when I kissed and ate her. The only thing I regretted was that I couldn't kill Ameen again. I straightened up the house and did as much clean up as I could on Patricia's body. My semen inside her would easily be dismissed. After all, I was her husband. I picked up my cell phone and made a call.

Dontay picked up on the second ring. "What's up, Mike?"
"Go get Quran and both of y'all come to my house."
"When?"
"Now!" I ordered.
"A'ight. Quran is on Howard Road. I'ma scoop him. We'll be there soon."
"Do that. Scoop Quran and come straight here. I'm waiting."

***

From the driveway, I watched Dontay Samuels and Quran get out of a silver Cadillac Eldorado ETC. The two teenagers were frick and frack. Always together. But no pair of dudes could have been more dissimilar in looks, styles, and demeanors. Quran was taller at five feet ten or eleven with a muscular build. Similar to his father. He also had the pecan pie complexion, dark curly hair, and light grey eyes. He was quiet, impulsive, smart, and fearless. Dontay was shorter. 5'8" and thick bordering on chubby. He was dark-skinned with acne, bubble eyes, and a short nappy afro.

They walked across the street and stood in front of me.
"What's up?" they both said in unison.
"Follow me," I instructed and led the way into the house.

My wife was where I had left her. On the couch. Still naked and still dead.

"What the fuck?" Dontay blurted out.

"Fuck you do to your wife, Mike?" Quran asked.

"I killed her. Got word that she was cheating with a cop and telling him all of our business."

"Our business?" Dontay asked.

"Yeah. Our business. She knew that the both of y'all be killing niggas for me. She knew about Carlos Trinidad and me getting the coke from them. Pillow talk is a muthafucka. She knew too much. Carlos's people found out. They called me."

"Damn, slim," Quran said. "Now what?"

"We move the fucking body, that's what. So stop with all the fuckin' questions and help me get her to the truck out back. I'll come back for her clothes."

***
One week later...

"You got a problem you need to solve, big homie." Jerome "Kenny" Woodard said as he dropped the brick of cocaine on the scale. The scale was on the middle console of the GMC Yukon.

"Is that right, slim?" I asked, about to pull out my gun. "What problem you talkin' about?"

Kenny put the brick of coke in a bookbag and slung it over his shoulder. Then he pulled a plastic Ziplock bag filled with money out of his dip. He passed the bag to me. "It's all there. As for the problem, it's the li'l young nigga Dontay. Shorty runs his mouth too much."

"Oh yeah? About what?"

"About a rack of shit that shouldn't be talked about."

"Slim, stop beating around the bush and just say what the fuck he been saying."

"He telling muthafuckas that you are the one that beat, raped, and killed your wife. Said you did it because she was hot and fucking with some police nigga. He's been saying other shit, too, but since your wife's been all over the news, I figured you'd wanna know that he's been talking about it. You know it ain't gon' be long before the wrong ears get wind of it."

"You right about that. I appreciate the heads up. That's definitely a problem. I'ma take care of it. The next time you cop, I'ma throw in a little something extra to show my appreciation."

"That's what's up, big homie. Thank you," Kenny said.

"Naw, thank you," I replied. Kenny exited the truck and disappeared around a corner. I picked up my cell phone and dialed Quran.

"Mike, what's good, slim?"

"Where you at? I need to holla at you."

"I'm in Oxford Manor, the complex on Bowen Road."

"Meet me at the ServQuick in twenty minutes."

"Bet. I'm on my way now."

***

By the time I pulled up to the ServQuick convenience store on Talbert Street, Quran was leaning on the wall eating a bag of chips. I parked the truck, hopped out, and approached him. We embraced.

"Let me ask you a question. How tight are you and Dontay?"

"Tight as can be. That's my man. You already know that. Why?"

"Let me ask you the question again——"

"I just answered the question."

"And I'm asking you again. How tight are you and Dontay?" I repeated.

"That's my man. I been knowing him all my life. He's from Dexter Terrace, but his mother lives on Sheridan Road. We went to the same Islamic schools and Masjids. His father n'em Muslim just like my family. He thorough. Ain't going for nothing and he gon' put that work in, but you know that already. That makes us pretty tight. Why, what's up?"

"You tight enough to do thirty years in prison for him?"

"Fuck no! Why you ask me that?"

89

"Because your man run his fuckin' mouth too much. Did you ever tell him about shit that me and you done did together? Don't lie!"

"Uh… I, uh…yeah, I did. I done told him a few things on top of all the shit that he already knows. All the shit that we done together. Why? What he say?"

"Naw, the question ain't what he say. It's what haven't he said? I was handling some business with a good man not too long ago and he told me that Dontay is running around telling people that I killed my wife because she was a rat and fuckin' a cop. Does that sound familiar?"

"Man…fuck! Stupid-ass nigga!"

"Exactly. And that ain't all he been saying. Nobody knows who really killed Tony Wells. I hope I don't need to remind you how dangerous shit gon' get for us if word gets out that it was you and that I sent you. You remember that second murder you caught, right?"

"Of course I do."

"Did you tell Dontay about it?"

"Don't think so, but I might have. I ain't sure."

"The only reason I started fuckin' with Dontay is because of you. You vouched for him. Said he was your man. Well, your man is either gon' get us locked up or killed. If we get locked up, do you think he'll hold up under pressure?"

"Of course, I think so, yeah!" Quran answered.

"In this life we live, you have to be sure, Quran. Which is it? You just said, 'of course, I think so, yeah.' I can't base my life and freedom on the unknown, the uncertain. Dontay been reckless with his mouth, and that makes him dangerous. And you already know what I do to muthafuckas who are a danger to me."

"I already know."

"So, let me ask you again. Are you tight enough with Dontay to do thirty or forty years in jail for him?"

"Fuck no!"

"You want to risk him ratting on us one day?"

Quran shook his head.

"I know that's your man, Quran, but all he had to do was keep quiet and he couldn't. He's a liability. Do you wanna take care of him, or should I?"

Quran ate the last of his chips. He balled up the empty bag and threw it down on the sidewalk. "I'ma take care of it. I got him."

***

Thirteen days later…

While I sat in the car and watched from down the street, Quran walked onto Dontay's mother's front porch and killed him. Then he calmly walked away.

***

The food slot on the cell door opened with a bang that broke my reverie and brought me back to the present time. I got up off the bunk and walked to the door. The CO passed two almost frozen box meals through the slot. I grabbed them and put them on the desk. Checking on my celly, I saw that Lil Man hadn't even stirred. His snoring continued. I went back to the door and watched the CO pass out box meals for dinner to every cell. Once that was complete, he went back into the office and sat down. I went to my spot and got out the cell phone. Once I powered it on, the voicemail icon on the screen lit up with a number. I had seven voicemails. I clicked on the text message icon and saw that I had ten new text messages. Quickly, I read each text. The voicemails, I'd listen to later. I remembered that I needed to get Sean Branch's number from Quran. I decided to call him second. My first call went to my sister.

Linda Carter answered her phone on the first ring. "Hello?"

"Sis, how are you? It's me."

"Hey, Mike! I'm good, and you?"

"Under the circumstances, I'm good as can be. Did Zin tell you about the affidavit that might free me?"

"She did. And if all goes well, you'll be home soon. I hope so, at least."

"Yeah, me, too. Let me ask you something, though."

"Ask me what? What's up?"

"What the fuck is going on with Zin?" I asked.

"What do you mean, Mike? Going on, how?"

"What do I mean? She came to see me earlier and I can tell that something about her was off. She wasn't her usual self. She asked me a rack of questions about old shit. Threw me off. Doesn't seem like it was the affidavit either. She had something on her mind, I could see it. Feel it."

"She seemed fine the last time I saw her. I couldn't see nothing strange with her. We laughed and had a good time yesterday. She's been going through some shit at work and she's tryna find a new place."

"A new place? Why? Her and Jermall are upgrading?"

"It's not Jermall, Mike. The man's name is Jermaine, and no, they're not upgrading. Zin moved out of the condo with him. She's been staying here with me."

"What happened with her and Jermaine?"

"She didn't tell you?" Linda asked.

"If she had told me, I wouldn't be asking you, would I?" I replied.

"Maybe she doesn't want you to know."

"Lin, would you stop bullshittin' and just tell me what's what?"

"Okay, but don't say nothing until she tells you on her own. Zin went home one day and found Jermaine in the bed with her boss, Jen."

"The fat one? In her bed with Jermaine?"

"Yup. So, she left him and the job. Girlfriend just opened her own law firm. She's looking for office space now. My niece has been holding up well. That's why I'm surprised that you think something is wrong with her. Zin out here living her best life, and she's bounced back fast after Jermaine. Her and that grey-eyed nigga are in love, I think…"

The breath in my chest deflated as my heart stopped momentarily. "What did you just say, Lin?"

"About Zin? Which part? Her one law firm? Her living her best life?"

"Naw, the other part about her bouncing back and the grey eyed nigga."

"Oh! Me and my big mouth. Zin didn't tell you about him, either, huh?"

"Tell me what?!"

"Zin has been dating Ameen's son. They been together for a few months now."

Anthony Fields

If You Cross Me Once 2

Chapter 12
JIHAD BASIR

I wiped dust off the tombstone. The picture of Tabu made into the tombstone was one that I had chosen. It was a good one. His smiling face stared back at me, just as it had the day his girlfriend Deja had snapped it while we were at Six Flags last summer. Quran had taken his on again/off again boo Tosheka. I'd taken Liv with me. The six of us parlayed in the large pool area for hours, laughed, joked, and had a lot of fun. At the time when Deja had taken the photo, Quran had just cracked on a fat chick whose big body was way too much for her small bikini. All of us had laughed, but Tabu laughed the hardest, and Deja captured his award-winning smile. When I saw the picture the day it was taken, I had Deja text it to my phone. I knew then that one day that picture would be worth something. Now it was forever etched in stone and would last once all of us were gone.

"I pray that Allah has made your grave spacious, li'l bruh," I spoke into the silence at the cemetery. "I wish that you were here. I can't understand why you did what you did, Tab. Why did you do it?" My tears started and wouldn't stop. "What the fuck were you thinkin'? You had to know that that shit would come out? There was no way to hide that you were gonna tell on Dave. Fuck was wrong with you? You know we didn't come up like that. Ameen Bashir didn't raise no rats. What made you do that wild shit? Huh?" I dropped to my knees and broke all the way down. I know what my brother did was against all the rules that I lived by, but he was still my brother. He was my little brother before all the street shit was taught to us. He was my brother before life changed and Quran became our father. Quran raised me, but I raised Tabu. He was my responsibility, and I failed him. He, in turn, failed us. And Quran took his life.

Anger welled up inside me again as it always did when I thought about Khitab being gone and the way he was taken out. How could one brother torture his baby brother in such a way, then leave him there hanging from a pipe like he was nothing, nobody? Images of

Tabu with his eye popped out was embedded in my brain. The hole in his face from the bullet that killed him was also seared into my head. Suddenly, I could hear Quran's voice in my head...

"What happened to Tab had to happen. Let's leave it buried with him. I don't ever wanna argue or beef with you about this again. You feel me?"
"I feel you, slim. It's buried with Tab. I love you, too, big brother. Til death do us part."

"Khitab was a rat. He broke the rules. His death was an honorable one," my conscience told me.

"I don't care. I don't care," I said to myself over and over again. "He didn't have to kill him. He was our brother. Our baby brother. Didn't that mean anything?"

When no answer to my question came, I cried heavily into my hands. My heart was torn into pieces, and I couldn't figure out how to put it back together. I thought that I would heal. I thought that I agreed with the reason for his death. I thought that I had moved on. I was wrong. The night I learned that Tabu was dead came to mind...

"Why didn't you tell me? When you first heard - well, read the papers, I mean?"
"Baby boy, I made the decision on the——"
"Just answer the question, Que! Why didn't you tell me when you first got the papers? Why wasn't I included in the decision-making process? Didn't my input mean something?"
"Jihad, I made the decision."
"But it wasn't your decision to make! Not on your own. He was my brother, too!"
"You really wanna know why I didn't tell you? I didn't tell you because I knew how emotional you'd be. I knew that you'd want to spare him. I knew how close you two were. I knew you'd be hurt, that you'd try and find a reason to get him off the hook. And most importantly, I didn't want to be influenced by the pain that I see in

your eyes right now. Besides, telling you wouldn't have changed the fact that Tabu snitched. He snitched on a friend of ours. He had——"

"You had no right!" I bellowed. "You had no right to kill my brother!"

"You had no right," I repeated to myself still remembering that night. "You had no right."

Turning around, I sat leaned up against Khitab's tombstone. My back was on the tombstone, my knees drawn up to my chest. "You had no right, Quran!"

"Our mother knew that Tabu was weak. He wasn't like us, she said. She knew it and we knew it. You knew it."

"Where are you going with this, Jihad? Are you justifying what Tabu did? I hope not. Because when Tabu became a rat, he became my enemy. He crossed Dave, he crossed you, and he crossed me. He gambled with his life and lost."

"He lost?" I spat. "He was our brother."

"Brother? Did you hear a word I just said? Tabu was a rat, baby boy, and a vicious one. He stopped being my brother the day he told on Dave. The man I killed wasn't my brother. He was my enemy. A rat anywhere is a threat to good men everywhere. What part of that don't you understand? Didn't you listen to our father? When a person crosses you once, they will cross you twice. Never give them that chance. How long do you think it would have been before Tabu told on one of us? A rat can't be trusted. Just because he was weak, doesn't mean that he should've been spared. You trippin' right now, baby boy. Clouded by emotion. You ain't thinking straight. All the muthafuckas that we killed, we didn't give a fuck why they told. We killed them because they told. What makes Tabu any different?"

"The fact that he was my brother made him different," I said to myself as I stood up and brushed myself off.

Anthony Fields

***

When I walked into the spot, Quran was there. He was laid out on the couch with a washcloth covering his eyes. His Timberland boots were set neatly to the side by the couch and his gun was on the coffee table inches away from his face. He pulled the washcloth from his eyes as I entered the spot, then covered his eyes again.

"What's up, Jay?" Quran asked.

"'Sup, big bruh?" I replied.

"Where you been at?"

"Riding around thinking."

"About what?"

"A rack of shit. But I'm good, though. What's up with you?"

"I'm cooling. Spent all day yesterday with Sean's lunchin' ass. That nigga's fucked up in the head. He's a real live serial killer, slim. That nigga cut off two niggas' heads yesterday and kept 'em."

"Stop what you doing, Que."

"Wallahi," Quran swore.

"Dayum."

"That's what I said."

"Don't tell me that all them bodies that been poppin' up everywhere been all him."

"You already know that nigga done came home and killed his baby mother and about fifteen niggas in like three weeks. I helped him bury some niggas and all that shit."

"Fuck he cutting niggas heads off for? And you said he kept the heads?"

"Yup. He cut two niggas' heads off and kept them A tongue, too. Said something about he always wanted to do that to niggas."

"Sean lunchin' like shit. Speaking of lunchin', your girl Toshika popped up over here yesterday," I told Quran. "Demanded that I let her in to make sure you wasn't here and all that shit."

"For real? Why you ain't call me and tell me that shit? How long did she stay?"

"Long enough to see that you wasn't here with no other bitches. And I did call you, but you never answered."

If You Cross Me Once 2

"My bad, baby boy. I got some shit on my mind, too. A rack of shit been eating at me. I found out yesterday that Pop was fuckin' a rack of bitches in the streets before he died."

"Pop? What pop is that?" I asked, confused.

"Our pops, nigga. Ameen Bashir. That's who. He was a lover of the ladies, it turns out. Nigga was cheating on Ma the whole time," Quran replied.

"Get the fuck outta here with that shit. Dad loved Mommy too much to do that shit."

"Again, that's what I said. But then I found out different."

"How, though?"

"Sean told me. He says that everybody in the streets back in the day knew that our father was a killer and a ladies' man. Pop was fuckin' his mother."

"Whose mother?"

"Sean's mother. He said that Pop was like a father to him. Taught him the killing game. Gave him his first gun and all that. He said that Pop introduced him to Mike. He started killing for Mike because our father told him to. After Pop died, he went to work strictly for Mike. Then he got caught up on that body."

"You believe that shit?"

Quran nodded. "Don't have a reason not to. I been around Sean a long time. He's a lot of things, but a liar ain't one of them. If he said it, it's true."

"Damn, I don't even know how to respond to that."

"No need to. Just file it in your head."

"If Sean knows all of that, he probably knows who killed Dad," I offered.

"I doubt that. If Sean knew who killed Pop, he would have been killed him, or at least told me so that I could kill whoever it was."

"I wish I knew who did it, bruh."

"Me, too, baby boy. Me too."

Anthony Fields

Chapter 13
GREG GAMBLE

"I'm tired of being your little secret, Greg."

"It's not a secret if you and I know."

Martin Mayhew slipped into his pants and adjusted his belt. "I'm talking to Greg the person right now, not Greg Gamble the perfect Mister United States Attorney. I'm going to need you to put your caring hat on right now."

"I don't have time to care, right now, Marty. I have to get to a meeting that's starting in an hour. And you know how traffic is on the beltway this early in the morning. Everything between us is good, fine… maybe better than good. It's great. No need to start making adjustments now."

"We've been together, what? Three years now? And nobody knows about me, Greg. I feel like I'm not living in my truth."

I laughed to myself. I couldn't believe Marty. "Marty, please don't lose yourself on me. You are an affluent, Millennial white male. The world is your oyster. You have a cushy job at Felix Strom Industries and all the amenities. Living in your truth? You sound like a fucking advocate for the LGBTQ community. We just spent the entire weekend together as if we were in coital and marital bliss and you think you're not living in your truth?"

"You know what I mean, Greg. I feel like we're hiding."

"Sometimes hiding is good. I'm the US. Attorney for DC," I told Martin.

"And Yvette Bowers is the mayor of DC and she's gay," he replied.

"But who knows that for sure? She never poses with any women or flaunts her sexual identification. She's the perfect example of why my life is good the way it is. We have a great life together, Marty. Please don't ruin it."

"And what if I just go public about us? Climb on my soapbox?"

"Then you'll experience the other side of me. A dark side that you don't want to see."

Anthony Fields

***
555 4th Street. NW.
Washington, D.C.

"Tell me the facts surrounding the Markal Mitchell case," I announced as soon as I was seated at the conference table.

Six assistant U.S. Attorneys sat around the table with me. I smiled at each one. Ari Weinstein, Susan Rosenthal, Davin York, Ann Sloan, Ian McNealy, and Jason Rapperport were the brightest minds that the U.S. Attorney's office had to offer.

"The decedent, Markell Mitchell, was shot outside of a shoe store at the East River Park shopping center. The shopping center is located in the 3900 block of Minnesota Avenue, in Northeast. MPD responded to the scene and found the victim unresponsive. He was pronounced dead at the scene. Cause of death, multiple gunshot wounds. Witnesses at the scene we've been interviewing say that it appeared that Mitchell was the intended target, so the ambush wasn't random. According to them, two men exited a vehicle that pulled to a stop near the victim, dressed in all black clothing. Both wore a face cover," Ian McNealy said.

"Did the witnesses say what type of vehicle?" I asked.

"Yes. The vehicle was described as champagne, tan, or gold in color. An SUV, either a Nissan or Infiniti. After shooting the victim, both men ran back to the SUV and it pulled off."

"Your investigation led to the man charged——"

"Dalvin Thomas. Dalvin James Thomas, twenty-seven. He has a home address of 4213 Eads Street in Northeast, which is only blocks away from the scene of the murder. Thomas is also - was also - an acquaintance of the decedent. They were indicted together on a murder a year and a half ago."

"Which murder? Was it here in DC?"

"It was. They were indicted on the Christopher Green murder that happened at the Minnesota Avenue Metro station. They were arrested, held at the jail, and indicted, but due to some unforeseen issues, the case fell apart. The charges were later dismissed, but not before Mitchell made several incriminating statements about

Thomas. At the charges were dismissed, Thomas was sent to Fairfax County, Virginia to face charges and Mitchell was released. According to our investigation, Thomas was released from custody in Virginia twenty-seven days before Mitchell was killed. He ended up doing time for a charge he pled guilty to. We have a man in custody for unrelated charges who contacted us and says that Dalvin Thomas killed Markell Mitchell because of the statement he made in the Green murder."

"Where is Thomas?"

"He's being housed at the Northern Neck Regional jail in Warsaw. We moved him to keep him away from our witnesses."

"Have you tried to interview Thomas, yet?"

"Interview him?"

"Yes, interview him. See if he'll implicate the second shooter. Or did you forget that witnesses said there were two shooters?"

Ian McNealy's face flustered. "Uh, no, I didn't forget that."

"Okay, your witness only gives you a reason for Thomas to want to kill Michell. It didn't take two people to kill one man. So, why was there a second shooter? And who was driving the getaway vehicle?"

"I see what you mean."

"Greg, if it's true that Thomas killed Mitchell for making statements, chances are slim that he'll make statements on his accomplices," Ari Weinstein added.

"Maybe you're right, Ari. Maybe not. Maybe Thomas wants to confess. Who knows. Ian, interview him and offer him a pre-indictment plea. Tell him about the people who are already talking."

"People?"

"Person is what we know. Your person already in custody that contacted us. Multiple persons is what you tell him. Threaten him a little with what you have and make up some stuff."

"What pre-indictment plea am I offering?"

"Offer him a cop to ten years with cooperation. Sixteen to twenty without cooperation. Tell him that if he cops without cooperation, we'll let his lawyer allocate it down to fifteen years, but he got to cop now. In the next thirty days. Let him know that even if we never get the SUV driver or the guy with him, if he goes to trial and loses, he's getting fifty years minimum."

Ian McNealy wrote hurriedly in his note book. "Got it, boss. Anything else?"

"That's all that I can think of. Get on it. Ari, what's on your agenda?"

Ari Weinstein opened a file folder in front of him. "I'm inundated with cases. The most important being the Jamal Johnson case..."

***
Later...

I was researching some case law when my secretary walked in.

"Mr. Gamble, an email just came in from the clerk of the court in Judge Kalfani's chambers. The judge is ready to rule on the motions filed in the David Battle case. He wants all parties in his courtroom tomorrow at nine a.m. The clerk needs to know of any scheduling conflicts as soon as possible."

"Shit!" I exclaimed. "I have something on the calendar for tomorrow at nine, don't I, Marge?"

"Yes sir, you have an eight o'clock scheduled for a meeting with Bill Nance from the ATF field office in reference to the Kevin Young conspiracy case. Then you have a nine o'clock meeting with the District Attorney from Prince George's County. Something about witnesses in the Mark Pray case. Then you have——"

"Marge, clear my schedule for tomorrow until after one. Call everyone and reschedule. I have to attend the Battle hearing."

"Do you want me to reply to the clerk in Judge Kalfani's chambers?"

"No, I'll do it. Thank you, Marge. Go ahead and make those calls for me," I said to dismiss my secretary. Once she was gone and the door was closed, I picked up the phone and dialed Judge Kalfani's chambers.

If You Cross Me Once 2

"Judge Gary Kalfani's court, how may I direct your call?" a male voice said.

"Todd, it's been awhile. How have you been?"

"Greg Gamble?"

"You remembered my voice, Todd. I'm flattered," I told the clerk.

"What can I do for you, Mr. Gamble?"

"So, it's Mr. Gamble now, huh? I need a favor, Todd."

"Uh...I...I...don't know, Mr. Gam——I mean, Greg," Todd stammered.

"Todd, the world is full of dark secrets. Would you like yours to get out?" I asked.

The line on the other end of the phone went deathly silent.

"Todd, are you still there?"

"I'm here. What do you need?"

"I need to know exactly how Judge Kalfani is planning to rule on the Battle case scheduled for tomorrow at nine a.m. And I need to know in the next hour or so."

"I'll call you back at this number in one hour." Click.

***

El Papi's Taco
Camp Springs, MD

The small Mexican restaurant in Camp Springs, Maryland had the best tacos that I ever tasted. I made sure to eat there at least once a week. The proprietor, Rudolph Zamora, stood at my table making small talk.

"Rudy, tell me how you get the Patriana's Red Tacos to taste so good?" I asked as I grabbed a taco from the fresh platter in front of me.

"Well, Greg, first I must tell you that Patriana is my wife. These particular tacos are a recipe that she created and perfected. I start by simmering briskets for hours in a stock pot. I remove the beef, but add the fat to reserves in a second pot for the consommé, which is the birria stew that doubles as a dipping sauce for tacos. There are seventeen ingredients..."

I knew that Rudy was still talking, but I had surreptitiously stopped listening. My attention was on the meeting with an old friend that I had been abruptly summoned to. The meeting needed to be private where no prying eyes could be. I suggested Papi's Tacos because of its location in suburbia, thirty minutes away from D.C.

"...and that's how I make the red tacos. I'm glad that you enjoy them."

"Thank you, Rudy, for having them. Tell your wife that they are delicious."

"I will, señor. Gracias," Rudy said and left.

I was on my second glass of Sangria and my third taco when my guest arrived. I stood up and embraced Gary Kolman.

Gary broke the embrace and sat down at the table. "These smell delicious."

"Please have some, then, or you can order your own meal. On me," I replied.

Gary removed his suit jacket and hung it on the back of his chair. "Wish I could, but I can't. They would ruin dinner with my wife in an hour or so, and Janine would never forgive me for that. Let me cut right to the chase and tell you why I asked to see you. Six years ago, for reasons still unknown to me, you did me a solid when you told me about Devon Hunt wearing a wire and the whole investigation of Mark Rachon and our office. Your heads up allowed me time and opportunity to dissolve my partnership with Mark before the Feds moved in on indicted him. That call you made back then may have single-handedly saved my career. Now, I got to return the favor.

"As you know, after Mark, I partnered with Abraham Shankle in his office. Do you remember one of Abe's clients named Michael Carter?"

"I do. I put him away for life on a murder beef."

"Correct. But here's what you don't know. Your eye witness - one of them, Maryann Settles - mailed to my office a three-page

If You Cross Me Once 2

affidavit recanting her testimony from the 1996 trial of Michael Carter. In a handwritten, detailed affidavit, she asserts that she was paid money to lie on Michael Carter and say that he killed Dontay Samuels. She alleges that her drug case was thrown out by you and Susan Rosenthal for her cooperation and deceit." Gary turned and reached into his inside jacket pocket to retrieve an envelope. He slid the envelope across the table. "Read it for yourself. I made a copy of the affidavit before passing it along to Jonathan Zucker, Carter's post-litigation attorney."

I opened the envelope and pulled out the affidavit. I read the first page and stopped. My blood simmered in my veins. I couldn't believe that almost seventeen years had passed and this situation was back and about to blow up in my lap.

"Settles says that she's willing to appear in court and face perjury charges. That can send her to jail and she knows it. And before you doubt its authenticity, don't. It's legit. I checked."

I smiled to disarm Gary Kolman. "If you knew how damaging the affidavit is, why didn't you simply turn it over to me and not Jon Zucker?"

"You don't think I entertained that thought? Well, I did. But I dismissed it when I realized that the affidavit arrived as certified mail. One of my paralegals had to sign for it. There was no ethical way that I could withhold a legally binding document that was certified as arriving at my office, from the post client's new attorney. I could be disbarred at a minimum and criminally charged at the most. Look, I did what I could, Greg. I copied the affidavit and now you have it. I suggest that you get on top of it before it gets on top of you. You remember what happened to Sam Howell, the prosecutor who put away the Newton Street crew." Gary stood up and put his jacket back on. "For years, I was in your debt. Now, we're even. Gotta go, Greg. Take care, buddy."

With that said, Gary walked out of the taco place.

***

Still in the parking lot of Papi's Tacos. I read the three-page affidavit again for the tenth time. "Shit!" I pulled out my cell phone and made a call.

"Hello?" a male voice answered.

"Donovan, it's me, Greg Gamble. I need your help."

"Need my help? How, Greg?" Donovan Olsen replied.

"I need everything you can find on two people. Christopher Settles and Maryann Settles. I'll text you everything that I have when I get back to my office."

"Okay, do that. I'll be waiting. Is this on book or off books?"

"Off. You still got that bogus account?!"

"Don't I always?"

"Send me the info again and I'll send money to it."

"The text should come through any minute now."

***

United States Attorney's office
333 4th St. NW

Susan Rosenthal swept into my office dressed in pajamas with a thin jacket over her top. Her perfume accompanied her into the room, one that I hated.

"Greg, what the fuck? It's late and I was just getting ready for bed when you called. What the hell couldn't wait until tomorrow morning? I had to leave——"

I pushed the envelope across the desk towards Susan.

"What the fuck is this?" she asked as she picked up the envelope.

"Read what's inside," I told her.

Susan read the three-page affidavit in its entirety before dropping down into the chair in front of my desk. The color drained from her face. She looked up at me. "Is this for real?"

I nodded. "Afraid it is. Gary Kolman copied it before passing it on to Jon Zucker. He gave me that copy today."

"She says that I made the payment to her."

"Susan, I know what it says."

"That happened sixteen years ago."

"I know that."

"Well, what are we gonna do?" Susan asked.

"I don't know. But this can open Pandora's box for us."

"For us?" Susan said and stood. "No, for you. That was standard operating procedure for you. Not for me. I only helped you with her...Maryann Settles. That one case. And I knew that I shouldn't have."

"So says the woman who's been fucking and helping Carlos Trinidad for years. Don't fuckin' get up on your high horse on me, bitch!" I said and stood, palms on my desk. "And don't look so surprised. Didn't think anybody knew, huh? Well, you thought wrong. One thing about me, Susan, is that I cover all the bases and I cover my ass. In 2003 when we indicted Kareemah 'Angel' El-Amin, DNA samples that matched the DNA taken from one of the murder victims was enough to go to trial. But then you happened."

"Me? What the fuck do you mean, I happened?"

"You gave Carlos Trinidad's people Fatima Muhammad's location and you got rid of the DNA samples. That's how Kareemah El-Amin beat the case."

Susan's facial expression went from anger, to shock, to defeat. "You can't prove that."

"You wanna bet?" I said with venom.

"You can't be serious!"

"Does your husband Grant know any of your secrets, Susan?

"Does anybody know yours, you fucking faggot? Or is that word politically incorrect these days? What do you like to be called these days, Greg? Queer?"

"It doesn't matter what you call me, Susan. Just remember to put 'boss' behind it, if you want to take my seat in a few years."

"If you know that I'm in bed with Carlos Trinidad, you do know what he's capable of if his name comes up in this, right?"

His name won't come up if you don't want it to. Help me bury this situation with Maryann Settles and all of our secrets stay buried."

Susan Rosenthal exhaled deeply and then retook her seat in the chair. "So, again I ask you, what are we going to do?"

If You Cross Me Once 2

Chapter 14
DAVID BATTLE
CENTRAL DETENTION FACILITY (D.C. JAIL)

"BATTLE! BATTLE! YOU GOT COURT!" the CO shouted into the cell.

"I hear you, CO. I'm up!" I replied from behind the sheet hanging from the ceiling out the front of the cell.

"Damn, they got you going to court this early?" Tiera asked.

I looked into the face of the beautiful young woman on my cell phone screen. "You nosy as shit. Ear hustling hard as hell."

"Ear hustling? Boy, bye. Whoever that was, was loud as shit."

"No bullshit. African correctional officer nigga was loud as shit. With his Desmond Tutu looking ass."

"Desmond who?" Tiera asked.

Laughing to myself, I realized that at twenty-three years old, Tiera didn't know who the famous African archbishop was. "Nobody, don't even trip. But they always do this. They get a nigga up for court at three in the morning."

"It's 3:17 a.m."

"I'm hipped. They get us up and send us down to RND and we stay down there until the Marshals pick us up and take us to the court building."

"I hope they let you come home."

"You too?" I said and smiled.

"I'm dead serious. You play too much," Tiera whined.

"I ain't playing, Tee. You think I like being in here? I'm doing my thing and all that, but I hate this funky-ass jail. I'm sick of this shit. All this shit. These creep-ass young niggas don't do nothing but pull their dicks out on bitches all day. This food nasty as shit. Them Aramark muthafuckas need a killing. The rest of these niggas rats, trannies, and suckas. I'm praying they let me out of this wild-ass jail. I wanna put my tongue in your pussy so bad. Let me see it again."

Tiera put her cell phone down between her legs. Pussy filled the screen.

"Damn, Tee, that pussy looks wet as shit."

"It is wet. Muthafucka stay wet."

"What the fuck? See what you made me do?" I pulled out my dick and stroked it, then put it in the phone's view so that Tiera could see it. She licked her lips as she watched me. "You got this joint hard as shit. I'm glad I ain't got no celly."

"I wish I could be your celly for one day. I'd suck that muthafucka all day. Deep throat that dick until I choke…"

"Stop what you doing, Tee. Talking like that and looking at me like that, you gon' make me——"

The cell door shook and then slid open.

"I can't help it. I miss you. I miss that dick."

I put my dick back in my boxers. "I gotta go. Gotta get ready for court. I'ma holla at you when I get back. Let you know what happened."

"You better. Bye, boy. I love you."

"Love you too, baby. I'm gone."

***

D.C. jail had dudes that cleaned up the tiers and unit all night. We called them detail dudes. My young nigga Antbone was one of them. I called him over as I made my way to the shower on the top tier.

"Here, put this shit up for me and I got you when I get back from court."

Antbone grabbed the sock with the cellphone, street knife and weed in it. "I got you, Unc. It's secure." Antbone left to put the contraband into a safe spot.

There were two showers on all four tiers. I got into the one closest to the mop closet and closed the curtain. The hot water massaged my tense muscles. I wanted – no, needed - to finish what Tiera started in the cell on the phone. I grabbed the muscle between my legs and handled my business while thinking about fucking Tiera the entire time.

If You Cross Me Once 2

Once I got that out the way, I thought about my current situation. The government was mad because all the witnesses in my case were dead. No witnesses, no case. They wanted to go to trial with grand jury statements and videotaped proffer sessions, something that I had never heard of before, something that I had never thought about when I told Quran to kill Landa and Tommy. I never knew who the last witness was. Finding out that it was Khitab, Quran's brother, was a helluva blow, one that Quran dealt with swiftly. Three people that I had once loved, all dead because of one death that had to happen. Three people who had been forced to betray me had all died because of Solomon "Manny" Robinson, a man who tested my gangsta and knew better …

"I'm shooting a hundred and betting a hundred."
"Shoot it," Chino said.
I locked the dice in my palm, then shook them around for a few seconds. I threw the dice out on the concrete. One landed on a two, the other a four. "Chino, bet a hundred on straight six, bet a hundred on the six, eight."
"Bet. You betting, Tom?"
"Yeah, I'm with Dave. Bet two on the six, eight," Tommy replied.
"That nigga lucky as shit," Jamaican Dex added. "I got five hundred he hit the six."
"Bet," Chino replied.
"Let me in on that," Stink said.
Jamaican Dex looked at Stink. "You with him or against him?"
"Against him. I'm tryna bet you five he don't six."
"Bet. Anybody else don't like the six?" *I asked.*
Lil Marcus Jones walked up to the crap game. "Dave, let me holla at you."
I rolled the dice out. They landed on a two and a three. "In a minute. Let me get this money." *I shot the dice again. Six. Four.* "Kobe Bryant, dice big two, four."
"That nigga robbed me, slim!" *Marcus announced.*

Everybody in the crap game turned to face Marcus. Lil Marcus was Marceles Duncan's little brother. He was a good little dude who was always looked out for because his brother was a gangster and in jail. Everybody liked Lil Marcus, especially me, and I was the one who fronted him coke to sell. "Who robbed you?"

"Manny!!" Lil Marcus said and his eyes filled with tears.

"Stay right there, slim. Let me make this number right quick," I told him. My concentration was off, but I shot the dice anyway. Three rolls later, I hit the six with double threes. I picked up all my money. "C'mon, Lil Marcus."

Me, Tommy, and Stink followed Lil Marcus. As we walked towards Sayles Place, Lil Marcus told us the story of what happened. Tommy and Stink never said a word to me. They knew what I was in. When we reached Sayles, Manny was nowhere to be found.

"Did he know that you was hustling for me, Lil Marcus?" I asked.

Lil Marcus nodded. "After he took everything, he said, now run and tell your man that."

"I'ma kill his bitch ass."

***

The next evening, I was standing on the homie Mann's porch talking to his niece Yolanda. I had fucked Landa once and liked it and was trying to hit again.

Tommy came up the back steps and called me. I walked over to him.

"What's up, cuz?" Tommy told me that Manny was nearby.

I walked back to Yolanda and told her that I was about to leave. She looked down the street and saw Manny and Khitab coming.

"I heard about what Manny did to Marceles' li'l brother. Everybody knows that that's your li'l man. Don't do nothing stupid out there, Dave," Landa said.

"I ain't gon' do nothing." I replied and left.

***

"Nigga, stop lying on your dick," Bo laughed and said.

"Lying on my dick? I'd rather lie on my mother," Manny said.

"LaTonya Snow ain't nobody, slim. Her pussy smells like fish."

Bo and Manny laughed at what Khitab said. Neither one of them paid any attention to me having walked up. I pulled out the gun in my waist and shot Manny in the head once. When his body fell, I went through his pockets. Everybody near us ran. Standing over him, I shot Manny again and then spit on him.

"You won't be robbing nobody else. Run tell that."

***

The handcuffs on my wrists were too tight. The metal was cutting into my skin. I glanced at the cuffs attached to the belly chain that encircled my waist. Then I could feel the shackles around my ankles. I felt like a captured slave. I looked out the window of the D.C. Department of Corrections van as it moved through the city. It appeared that a lot had changed in the year and change, I'd been in jail. I wondered how much more things would change before I was allowed to go free. For some reason, my homie Mann came to mind. Maybe it was because I had killed two of his witnesses to get him home after he'd killed a dude in Howard Gardens a few years ago. I remembered that Mann had been killed himself a month or so ago. Although no one told me, I knew that Quran had killed Mann. If Quran was nothing else, he was smart, cautious, and concise. He'd known without having to be told that once Landa was killed, Mann had to follow. Mann would never rest until he found out who had killed his niece. If all went well, I owed it all to Quran. And to me, that was a gift and a curse.

A song on the radio got my attention and I rapped along with it.

"…racing my men and mountain climbing / for about ten diamonds / twenty-five thousand a piece / fuck streets / I'm tryna own an island / forget about wildin' / try riding in a car that be gliding /

115

if I showed you where I lived / you would think I was hiding / sling bricks to chicks who don't speak English / wake up in Trinidad, like fuck it, I'm rich / come back live on set / private jet / it's the key to life / money, power, and respect / have you eating right / money, power, and respect / it's the key to life / money, power, and respect / have you eating right / money, power, and respect / help you sleep at night / you'll see the light…"

Money. Power. Respect. Getting to the money was easy. Respect came with the fact that everybody knew that my gun game was mean. All the witnesses coming up dead bred even more respect. It was the power that always seemed to elude me, real power in the streets, the power that Quran possessed. The power to make even the toughest of men bow down, the power that came with loyalty, respect and love from the entire city. It was a well-known fact that Quran had been killing gangstas since he was like twelve or thirteen. That afforded him the ability to dictate to men everywhere. His brother Jihad was strong in his own right. He commanded a crew of young niggas that were vicious and dangerous, a crew that would kill instantly if he gave the word. And Quran commanded them all. Quran had it all, the complete trifecta. Money, power, and respect. And although we were close and he was loyal to my cause, I couldn't deny the fact that my life had a glass ceiling with Quran in it. I needed to either find a way to remove the glass ceiling or remove Quran.

***

"Your Honor, the statements of the deceased must be considered. All the witnesses would be here had they not been made unavailable by the defendant."

Zin Carter stood up immediately. "Your Honor, I object to this accusation lodged by U.S. Attorney Gamble. There is no scintilla of evidence that links my client to the tragic deaths of Yolanda Stevens, Thomas Caldwell, or Khitab Bashir. The case law that USA Gamble is citing is totally inapposite to the case at hand."

If You Cross Me Once 2

"Your objective is noted, counselor. Please proceed, USA Gamble," Judge Gary Kalfani said.

"In the interest of justice, Your Honor, this court must take into account what transpired with Tomas Caldwell, now deceased, and a family member of the defendant. Thomas Caldwell met with government officials on not one, not two, not three, but on at least six different occasions. And on every one of these occasions, he reiterated his concerns for his safety. Thomas Caldwell said, and I quote, that 'the defendant, David Battle, had several dangerous friends.' He even went as far as to name one of these men as Q.B. It was later determined that Q.B. is a thirty-four-year-old man named Quran Bashir. Call records retrieved from the phone system at the D.C. jail reveal that several of the defendant's calls reveal messages sent to a person named Quran."

"Your Honor, again, I object to this. The defense has received no notice of the government's intention to cite phone calls from the D.C. jail."

"Defense counsel Carter, the US. Attorney is positing a theory and citing phone records that you and your client knew were fair game. There's a recording on the phone that lets all users know their calls are being monitored. Continue, Mr. Gamble."

"Several calls were made to men who cannot be identified. Messages were sent. Coded messages. Thomas Caldwell had a very real fear for his life due to his assistance to the government. As mandated by the laws of this court, names were given to defense counsel. And now Mr. Caldwell is dead, killed as he left a nightclub."

"Your Honor, this is getting outrageous. United States Attorney Greg Gamble knows better than anyone in this courtroom that Metropolitan police detectives investigated the murder of Thomas Caldwell and concluded that his murder was the result of a robbery gone bad. To imply that my client ordered the death of Thomas Caldwell is wrong and unfair. We object to all implications that David Battle caused the unavailability of these three witnesses."

"Counselor Gamble, I've noticed that the name of one of the witnesses who was killed, his last name was Bashir. And you've just posted a theory of witnesses possibly being killed by a friend of

117

the defendant, a man named Quran Bashir. To your knowledge, would these two men be related?!" Judge Kalfani asked.

"Uh...Your Honor, that would be correct. Our records reveal that Khitab Bashir is the younger brother of Quran Bashir."

"And you're positing this theory that this man Quran Bashir killed his own brother?"

"We can't positively say that anyone killed any of the witnesses in this case. I'm just making this court aware of Thomas Caldwell's concerns for his safety and his words that he believed he'd be killed by friends of the defendant, namely Q.B., who is Quran Bashir. Your Honor, if I may, I'd like to point out another issue. We have a detective here today to testify to the statements that the defendant made the night he was arrested on gun charges."

"Objection, Your Honor. The Rossir letter sent to defense counsel clearly states that the defendant made no statements," Zin Carter interjected and said.

"Your Honor," Greg Gamble argued, "the government wasn't made aware of the statements the defendant made to law enforcement until after the first Rossir letter was sent out. A second Rossir was sent out when we learned that David Battle told Detective Harold Johnson, and I quote, 'Y'all ain't got nothing on me. Your witness recanted.' These statements, in conjunction with the unavailability of Thomas Caldwell, who did try to recant his grand jury statements, proves the government theory that the defendant actively pursued avenues to get the witness not to cooperate with the government."

Judge Gary Kalfani banged his gavel. "I've heard enough. I'm ready to make my ruling in this matter. In the interest of justice..."

***

"Did I tell you right? Didn't I tell you to have faith in me?" Zin Carter said as soon as she walked into the holding cage area behind the courtroom. She walked up to the bars and high-fived me.

Smiling, I said, "You did that. I can't front. You did your thing out there. I'm glad I agreed to retain you when you left Locks and Wentz."

"Damn, it feels good, don't it? We beat that muthafucka. Greg Gamble out there mad as shit. Did you see the look on his face when Judge Kalfani denied their motion? He looked constipated, like he hadn't shitted in weeks and his stomach hurts."

"I gotta say thanks again, Ms. Carter."

"Don't mention it, David. At the end of the day, like I told you, they couldn't get around the 6th amendment, the confrontation clause issue. An accused has the right to be able to cross examine the witnesses against him. And you can't cross examine paper and videos. The judge had to deny their motion or get reversed on appeal had you lost at trial. He decided to man up and do the right thing now. I respect him for that. I really thought he was going to side with the government. I was wrong."

"I'm glad that you were. So, what happens now?"

"This was a pretrial matter. Without witnesses, obviously there's no case. In the next seventy-two hours, the government has no choice but to concede and dismiss all charges against you. But you still have the gun charge in front of Judge Berger. It's a simple CPWL. It's gonna be hard to beat because the Judge ruled at the suppression motion that the traffic stop was legal due to the traffic violation. The gun was under your seat and it had your fingerprints on it. That's the dilemma. Greg Gamble is not gonna let Ian McNealy, the prosecutor in the case, offer you any cops. He's mad about this case. You'll have to sit for a while."

"Damn, that's fucked up."

"Heather Pinckney is your lawyer on that case. Maybe she can get the government to play fair. You've been in jail for almost seventeen months. With the right Judge, if you can petition for a different one, what you have in is time served. Let me get with Heather Pinckney and get back to you. After this case is dismissed, just be cool and don't get into any trouble at the jail. You hear me?"

"I hear you. I hear you."

"A'ight. I'ma get you out of jail. Trust me."

"I trust you. And one more thing. I need you to take on a case for me."

"Take on a case? Whose case?" Zin Carter asked.

"My lil man Antbone. His real name is Anthony Williams. Been in since he was sixteen fighting some bodies. He told me bits and pieces about the case, and I think you can get him off," I told her. "His public defender is some shit."

"He's on the juvenile tier?"

"Naw. He's eighteen now and on the adult block with me."

"Who's his lawyer, now?"

"Malachi Chu."

"Never heard of him. Let me look up his case and see what's going on and if I think I can come in and win, I'll let you know. I'm not doing his case pro bono, so who's gonna foot the bill for his defense?"

"I am. Since you just started your own firm, I'm sending you clients. I'ma pay you for shorty. Just don't hit me over the head."

"I got you. Just let me look into it first."

Chapter 15
ZIN

The Finebaum building on 18th and M Street in Northwest was a perfect place to open my firm. The suite was spacious and immaculately kept. I knew that I wanted the suite as soon as I saw it. I got in the elevator, still exhilarated by my win in court over Greg Gamble. A smile crossed my face as I remembered the constipated look of annoyance when Judge Kalfani denied all of the government's motions. Greg Gamble was used to winning, to getting his way in courtrooms. Just to watch his body sag in defeat was almost orgasmic. Then I thought about his words to me a week ago in the hallway at the court building ...

"...I found a way then to produce other witnesses and secure a conviction against your father. I will repeat history in this same courtroom by finding a way to convict your client. David Battle will never see the light of day again as a free man. Not as long as I'm alive and breathing..."

I made a mental note to visit David at the jail and tell him what Greg Gamble said. He needed to know that his case was personal to Greg Gamble and that getting him out of jail was gonna be a steep hill to climb. I thought about everything I had already told David earlier. Maybe I had already made that point to him and I was just being paranoid. Or scared. I also made a note to self to go and see Jon Zucker as soon as possible. I wanted to ask him the exact same questions that I had asked my father on the visit over the weekend. Just as the elevator chirped and the doors opened, I thought about Quran.

"Good afternoon, my name is Zinfandel Carter. I have a one o'clock appointment with Mr. Finebaum."

The receptionist in Harvey Finebaum's office reminded me of Jessica Alba. She was beautiful. "I love your first name, Ms. Carter."

"Thank you very much. My mother thought her favorite wine would be a great name for her only daughter."

"Smart lady. Mr. Finebaum will be with you shortly. Please have a seat."

I found a chair in the waiting area and sat in it. My mind immediately went to Quran and my mother's letter. Disgust slowly crept into my gut. Then my inner voice said, *Patience, Zin. Patience. Stick to the script. Master your emotions and stay the course.*

"Ms. Carter, Mr. Finebaum is ready to see you now."

I was led down a hall to the office at the corner. The door was open. As I walked in, Harvey Finebaum stood behind his desk. He was short and portly, but stylishly dressed. His hair was thin on top and completely gray. He reached out his hand for me to shake. "Zinfandel Carter. Nice to meet you. I'm Harvey Finebaum."

"Hello, Mr. Finebaum. It's nice to finally meet you." I replied.

"Oh, stop it. The pleasure is all mine. I have a friend at the Superior Court who speaks highly of you. He actually called you a shining star in criminal defense law. I'm glad that you chose us to facilitate your first law office. Did you like the suite?"

"I did. As a matter of fact, I loved it, and would like to move in as soon as possible."

"Great. How does today sound?" Harvey Finebaum asked.

"Today sounds like music to my ears, sir. Thank you," I responded.

"Okay. All that will be required is a $5000 security deposit and three months' rent in advance. Your lease will be a twenty-four-month lease with all the usual penalties if you should need to break the lease before twenty-four months. The monthly rent will be twenty-three hundred dollars, bringing your total to $11, 900. Are you prepared to pay that amount today, Ms. Carter?"

I went into my purse and pulled out my Navy Federal debit card. "I am, Mr. Finebaum."

"Splendid. Sally has the necessary paperwork all ready for you to sign and then she'll take you to my finance office, where you can make that payment. Welcome to the Finebaum building, Ms. Carter.

Sally will also give you the security codes for your suite and extra keys."

"Thank you, Mr. Finebaum."

***

Quran silently walked through the suite and checked out every inch of it.

"Quran, say something. Do you like it?" I asked.

"Of course I do. This is a nice spot, Zin. You can make the big room your office. You can have a small office for an assistant or paralegal. That room over there can be a small storage area. This out here can be the waiting area. You can line chairs up along the wall over there. You've got a little kitchen area and a full bathroom. I like it."

"Glad to hear that, because I like it a lot. Didn't know you had interior decoration in your blood."

"There's still a lot about me that you don't know," Quran said.

Ain't that the gospel truth. "I can only imagine. But I think I'ma take your advice and do everything like you just said it. I'ma need to shop for furniture and appliances. I need to find movers…"

"I can help with that. My brother and his men can help."

"Thank you, but I'd rather have professionals. The building has Wi-Fi, but I still need a cable provider, a landline phone…"

"And by doing all of that, I won't be seeing you again until next week. See, Zin, that's the bullshit I'm talking about."

"Bullshit? Quran, I'm a professional woman with a career that I worked hard for. A career that I love. I have priorities and responsibilities. I have appointments and a lot of other shit that I have to do, shit that Jen and Nikki did while I worked for them. Since I now work for myself, those things have to get done by me. I have a life outside of Quran Bashir. You knew that when we started this, so don't start acting crazy now. I been busy as hell the last few days and I have a lot of work to do in the upcoming weeks. I have to get this suite put together. I have to find a condo of my own——"

"You can live with me at my condo," Quran interjected.

Ignoring Quran, I continued, "I need to check on my father's case, I have motions to file, clients to visit, research to do, new clients to see, an upcoming trial in federal court, and I'm trying to get David out of jail. So excuse me if you don't get to see me as much as you'd like."

The look on Quran's face was one of hurt and disappointment. "How is that coming along?"

"How is what coming along, Quran?"

"Getting Lil Dave out of jail."

"It's coming. Today was the day for his hearing. The judge on his case ruled against the government, denying them the chance to use the witness statements at trial. All three of the witnesses are unavailable and therefore can't be cross-examined, so the government has no other choice but to dismiss all charges. That should happen in the next few days."

"That's good to hear. I know Lil Dave is happy."

"He is, but he's not. He still has the gun charge to fight. He's held in that case, too, so even when the charges in Solomon Robinson's murder are dropped, he's gotta stay at D.C. jail."

"Damn! I forgot all about the gun charge."

"Well, we haven't. David and I. I have been working hard and I still have a lot of work to do, so ease up on a sista. My not being able to be with you lately is not intentional."

"You're right," Quran acquiesced. "I just miss you. That's all."

"A-a-a-w-w! Ain't that special," I said and moved closer to Quran. "Is it me you miss? Or is it my pussy, head, and tight ass that got you feeling neglected?"

Quran covered the ground between us that was left. Our faces were inches apart when he said, "You have a really dirty mouth. Someone needs to fill it with soap."

I looked Quran straight in the eyes and replied, "I'd prefer dick."

"Are you tryna start something right now, Zin? Because if you are, it's working."

If You Cross Me Once 2

I reached out and grabbed Quran's Hugo Boss jogger pants, reached inside, and grabbed his dick. I rubbed my thumb around the head. "Are you?"
"Is that door over there locked?"
"I don't know and I don't care."
"Zin, you gon' make me fuck the shit outta you in here."
"Before I ran into you, I was a good girl. A nice and sweet lawyer. But now I can't help being bad around you. My dirty mouth is all your fault." I dropped to my knees and put Quran's dick in my mouth. As I sucked it, I could hear music playing in my head ...
"...is it bad, bae / I never made love / no, I never did it, but I sure knew how to fuck / I'll be a bad girl / I'll prove it to you / I can't promise that / I'll be good to you / 'cause I had some issues / I won't admit / I'm not hiding it / but at least I can admit / that I'll be bad to you / I'll be good in bed / but I'll be bad to you..."

Quran gripped my shoulders and fed me his dick. But then, without notice, he pulled back until my mouth was empty. Quran pulled me up off my knees. He moved me back to the wall and then lifted me into the air. His arms locked under my legs, forcing them open.
"Quran, what are you doing?!"
"What does it look like I'm doing?"
My back was against the wall, my hands rubbed Quran's hair. Quran's face was inside my skirt.
"Quran, stop!" I protested.
Quran's tongue was forceful. Like a finger, it dipped inside my panties and moved them aside. Then his tongue was inside me. I leaned my head back and bit my bottom lip to muffle my moans. I felt turned on in a way that I never had. I was in a position that I had never been in. I felt helpless. I felt powerless to stop Quran's tongue from assaulting my inner spot and my clit. I tapped the wall lightly. I was submitting as if inside a UFC octagon. I wiggled in Quran's embrace. It felt so good that tears came to my eyes.
"Quran...Quran...please stop! Ooooh... shit!"

My pleas fell on deaf ears as Quran continued his assault on me. He was determined to taste my sweet nectar, and after a few more minutes of pure ecstasy, I didn't disappoint. I came hard and loud all over Quran's face. I thought that our tryst was over, but I was wrong. Quran was a man of his word. He did exactly what he said he was going to do. He fucked the shit out of me on the suite's carpeted floor and then up against the wall. Quran's tongue licked on my neck as he fucked me facing the wall. He stood behind me. My skirt was at my waist, my panties long discarded. My shirt and bra were wet with perspiration. I had cum on Quran's dick twice already and he knew it, but yet he soldiered on. Then, without warning, Quran took his soaking wet dick out of my pussy and forced it into my ass. The pain was unbearable at first, but as time passed, it became pleasurable pain. I cried out to Quran to go slow, to be gentle. But he ignored me. I gave in completely to the strange feeling that I had grown to love. And the next thing I knew, I was cumming again.

***

"Look at this shit," I said to Quran as I washed up in the suite's bathroom. "You got me in here washing up with hand soap and my panties. I gotta go the rest of the day with no panties on."

Quran sat on the toilet, naked from the waist down. He laughed. "You gon' be a'ight. That pussy need to breathe some fresh air. Gimme them joints when you finish."

"What? Hell no! You are not washing your dick off with my panties. No."

"Why not? You already using them like a washcloth. Let me go next."

"I see your point. I should be mad at your ass, but I'm not."

"Mad at me, for what?" Quran asked.

"Because I didn't get a chance to finish sucking that dick. My pussy and butt sore as hell and cum gon' be running out of me until I get some tissue. Since I ain't gon' have on no panties, it's gon' run down my leg."

"Good. At least you'll think about me all day. And you can finish sucking this dick tonight. Am I gonna see you?"

"Probably. I got a few more things to do before my day ends, but I'll say that the chances of us spending the night together are good. But we ain't fucking. That's for sure. All you're getting is some head."

"That's cool with me."

"I already know it is, with your nasty self."

"Zin, tell me you love me."

"I love you, Quran."

"Good. Now hurry up and give me the panties and soap."

"Here." I passed Quran the soaped-up panties. "Shit smells like the D.C. jail bathroom in here."

Quran cracked up, laughing.

I laughed until I remembered something I needed to tell Quran. "Damn, speaking of D.C. jail, you need to be careful before you end up over there."

"Be careful? And end up over where?" Quran asked.

"You heard me. Over the jail. I meant to tell you this when I first saw you, but I kinda got distracted by how good you look, then I ended up in the air on the wall. Thomas Caldwell——"

"Black Tommy. Dave's cousin. What about him?"

"Before he died, he was cooperating with the cops for months, wavering back and forth on whether or not he wanted to keep telling. He told the government that you were going to kill him if it ever got out that he was assisting the government."

"Me? He said I was gonna kill him?"

I nodded. "Yeah, you. As a matter of fact, your name came up quite a bit at that hearing today. According to Gamble, Thomas Caldwell didn't call you by name. He used your initials. Greg Gamble read Thomas Caldwell's statements to the judge. In those statements, Caldwell said, 'Dave has very dangerous friends who'll kill for him, namely a man named Q.B.' It was Greg Gamble who said that their investigation revealed that Q.B. was Quran Bashir."

"Damn, my whole government, though?"

"Yup. His words to the judge exactly. Verbatim."

Quran was washing his dick and balls, but stopped mid-wash. He turned to face me. "So, does that mean that I'm under investigation now?"

Chapter 16
QURAN

"I'm not sure. He said that in open court. So, maybe not. Usually when the feds are investigating someone, they do everything in their power to keep it a secret from their target."

"Maybe it's not the feds," I said as I continued to wash up.

"Maybe, maybe not. From what I know about law enforcement in D.C., when a crew, group, gang, or any person is under investigation for robberies, gun trafficking, murders, drugs, carjackings, banks, it's the feds that come in and investigate. Local homicide will investigate a murder, maybe even two, but I think three murders of witnesses would justify the feds coming in. It could be either or it could be none of the above. I'm just telling you what was said in court today. It's never good for any of them government agencies to have your name."

"True dat."

"And another thing: be careful with them D.C. jail phone calls. Their phones are monitored and the government attorneys are experts at manipulating those calls to fit whatever agenda they want them to. Your name came up about jail calls, you having spoken to David."

"But why does that even matter? Whether or not I spoke to Dave on the phone? We're friends. They know that two friends conversating——"

"C'mon, Quran, think. The government believes that David ordered the deaths of all of his witnesses. They can't prove it, but they definitely believe it. They've been arguing that to the judge for weeks now. Especially now that Judge Kalfani has ruled against them, they're going to want to pursue someone for those murders, and the likely person is you, because Thomas Caldwell was afraid of Q.B."

"I hear you loud and clear, but they wasting their time with them jail calls. I'm too careful for that. I never talk reckless on the phone about anything."

"Good. Keep it like that," Zin said and fixed her clothes.

Once I was done and dressed, we left the bathroom together. Zin found her heels and slipped them on. The wet panties, I kept.

"What are you going to do with them panties?"

I embraced Zin and kissed her passionately. "I'm a let them dry in the car by the air vent. Then I'ma keep them as a reminder of what we just did."

"I'm trying to forget the last part, but I can't because my ass is hurting. You keep that up and I'ma have PTSD." Zin kissed me again. "See you later, alligator. Thanks for breaking in the new suite."

"Anytime, baby girl. Anytime. Call me when you ready to meet later."

"I will."

***
1351 Howard Road

As soon as I walked in the door of the spot, I could hear the sounds of loud sex. Moans, cries of ecstasy, my brother Jihad's voice. Smiling to myself, I sat on the couch to rest. The news was on T.V.

"…city under siege, Fox News at four. I'm Maria Wilson. Today's top story is again crime in our nation's capital. Law enforcement officials are preparing to meet with the mayor and the city council to discuss initiatives to lessen gun violence and the proliferation of guns on the streets. Three weeks ago, the bloated and disemboweled body of a woman was fished out of the Potomac River near the Wharf. The woman was identified as forty-two-year-old Raquel Dunn. Authorities are still investigating her murder. No arrests have been made.

"In other news, the identities of the two men shot and killed in a house on Third Street in Southeast days ago have been revealed. Authorities say that both men were shot, but one of the men was also decapitated. His head has not yet been found. They were identified as Artinis Winston and Byran Clark. Sources close to the scene have told CUS Fox News that both men testified last year against a group of men who were convicted of trafficking drugs from a barbershop on Martin Luther King Jr. Avenue in Southeast.

"In other news, the two men found shot to death on Orleans Place in Northeast yesterday were identified as thirty-seven-year-old Miguel Harris and Jeffrey Vinson. D.C. police have no suspects or motive as to why the two men were killed. A third man is at a local hospital with life threatening injuries…"

"You like this dick?" Jihad's voice called out.

"Yes…yes…oh, yes!" the female voice responded.

"Whose dick is bigger?"

"Huh?"

"Whose dick is bigger? Me or my brother's?"

"Yours! Yours! Yours!"

"Who fucks you better? Me or him?"

"You! Oh, Jihad…fuck me!"

The voice of the female sounded familiar. Getting up off the couch, I crept towards the bedroom door. The door was closed, but not all the way. I pushed the door a little to see who the female was that Jihad was fucking. When I was able to see her face, I smiled. My old flame Tosheka was on the bed on all fours. Her fists gripped the comforter on the bed as she bit down on a mouthful at times. Tosheka was naked from the waist down. Her pants and panties were huddled around her ankles. Her socks were multicolored. I could see her Prada tennis shoes near the bed. Tosheka's shirt rose up her back to reveal the tattoo she had there with "Quran" on it. Jihad's hands gripped Tosheka's waist as he pounded into her. I laughed to myself, turned, and went back to the couch. I laid down and closed my eyes. I had never loved Tosheka the way that she claimed to love me. We were two totally different people. I had no ill feelings about her giving her pussy to Jihad. Honestly, I had no feelings at all. There was only one woman on my mind, one woman that had my heart. As I listened to Jihad fuck Tosheka, I thought about Zin.

***

"Quran, bruh, how long you been here?" Jihad asked.

I opened my eyes and saw him standing over me. Tosheka's was behind him looking stupid. "Long enough. Why? What's up?"

"Big bruh, I...I...it ain't——"

"Jay, I'm tired as shit, baby boy. You don't owe me no explanations. I don't give two fucks about you fucking Tosheka. She's a thot. I always knew that. That's why I never wifed her."

"Uh, I'm standing right here. Whatever you gotta say, Que, you can say to me." Tosheka said sassily.

"You heard what the fuck I just said. I don't give two fucks about you giving that pussy to my brother, so y'all ain't gotta be sneaky. Life's too short for that."

"Fuck you, Quran!"

"No thanks. That's for Jihad to do now. Especially since he fuck you better and his dick bigger than mine," I said and laughed. "Fuck outta here. I'm going to sleep for a little while. I'll holla at you when I get up, Jay, so make sure that you are somewhere nearby." I closed my eyes.

"Quran, I'm sorry!" Tosheka exclaimed. "I didn't mean to! I love you, Quran! I only did that to get your attention. To make you mad. You've been acting so funny lately. Jihad was there. I really wanted you. I'm sorry. Quran! Please talk to me!"

I opened my eyes to see Tosheka standing over me with tears running down her cheeks. I turned my back to her and went to sleep.

***

"Hello?" I groggily said into the phone.

"Que, it's me, Kiki. Just wanted to let you know that I'm flying back to the East Coast tomorrow. What do you want me to do?"

"Want you to do? I'm lost, remind me?"

"Que, are you asleep?" Kiki asked.

"Damn, I was. But I'm up now. What were you saying, Kiki?"

"Are you coming to Virginia, or am I stopping in D.C.to see you?"

If You Cross Me Once 2

I swung my legs off the couch and sat up. I shook my head to clear it of the cobwebs that stood between sleep and being awake. I thought about Kiki's question and then about how good her sex was. As bad as I wanted to curve Kiki, I couldn't do it. She was spontaneous, wild, and fulfilling. My dick got hard just thinking about Kiki. "Go ahead and detour in the city. Stop at Reagan National and get a room at the Courtyard hotel nearby. Pay for everything and I'ma reimburse you in cash tomorrow. Cool?"

"Yeah, but you don't have to reimburse——"

"I want to." I stopped Kiki and said, "This pit stop is on me."

"If you insist. Can't wait to see you, Que. Bye."

"A'ight. Same here. Call me when you're here."

I ended the call. Just then Jihad walked into the spot. He sat in the love seat across from me.

"I don't have to worry about you killing me, do I?" Jihad asked.

Looking at my watch, I saw that it was a little after seven in the evening. I grabbed my phone from where I'd just tossed it and checked to see if Zin had called. She hadn't. But there were several missed calls from Tosheka and two from Mike Carter. "Why would you ask me some stupid-ass shit like that, Jay?"

"I don't know. You might feel like I crossed you by fucking Tosheka and you know how the saying goes. If you cross me once——"

"I don't feel like you crossed me, baby boy. Tosheka was never my woman. We were just fucking. I care about her, but she can fuck who she wants. I never gave no fucks about who she gave that good pussy to. I always fucked who I wanted to and she did her. Just because she went and got my name tattooed on the small of her back didn't change how I felt about her. That was her dumbness for thinking we were exclusive, if she thought that. I haven't touched Tosheka since I been with Zin. I been ducking her. You know that. So, since she can't have me, she fucked you. Why would I be mad at you? Or feel like you crossed me? Tosheka's a thot."

"A thot who's outside sitting in her car. She's been out there since earlier when you turned over on her. She wants to see you."

"I'm busy," I told Jihad.

133

"A'ight. I feel that. I'm glad you not fucked up at me, because shorty came on to me. Got real aggressive after we smoked some loud. Took off her clothes and forced me to fuck her."

"Forced you to fuck her? Stop what you're doing, baby boy." I laughed.

"No bullshit, Que. I'm the victim in all of this. Are you sure you cool with it?"

My phone vibrated. The caller was Tosheka. I ignored the call. "Stop fuckin' playing with me, Jay. I said I don't care and I mean that."

"Gotta check, big bruh, because niggas who cross you end up dead."

"Well, don't ever cross me, then. On another note, we might have a problem."

"Problem? What kinda problem?"

"That bitch nigga Black Tommy told them people that Dave had dangerous friends that kill for him. Mentioned me to them. Told them that I was gonna kill him if word ever got out that he was snitching. Zin said that Tommy called me Q.B. and it was the government, the United States Attorney nigga Greg Gamble, who said that Q.B. was Quran Bashir."

"There's one U.S. Attorney, right? For D.C., I mean?"

"Yeah. Greg Gamble is the top dog. Everybody else in the building is AUSA's, or assistant U.S. Attorneys."

"So, the top dog knows who you are?"

I nodded my head.

"Big bruh, that is a problem. So, what do we do about it?" Jihad asked.

"At the moment, nothing. I'm still tryna figure it out. I ain't never been locked up for nothing since that assault when I was seventeen. That shit got dismissed. I can't figure out how them people got my name unless it was Landa or Tabu. Or maybe it's somebody else talking to them that we don't know about. Have any of your men gotten locked up lately?"

"Naw. And if they had, all of them niggas I fuck with know better."

If You Cross Me Once 2

"Tabu knew better, too, but he talked anyway. Find out if somebody on the team got arrested in the last three months and ain't talkin' about it. All this time I been thinking that I been flying under the radar. At least, now I know better."

"Stop what you're doing, big boy. I just really thought about what you're saying. I get it that what Zin told you fucked you up, but come on...really? How the fuck you really thought that you was under the radar? All these years, you been putting in work, and all these niggas that know both of us been getting locked for years. You really just figured out that niggas is going to them precincts and down 555 Fourth Street and they might be saying your name? Look at what Tabu did. You don't think niggas ain't been bartering for their freedom off of you and me? Bruh, you gotta already know that them people got a file somewhere with our names in it. They got a file on our father somewhere, too, and Pop never went in on a body either. We knew that because Ma told us that at Mike Carter's trial, Pop's name came up repeatedly. You been crushing shit for almost twenty years and you really surprised that them people know who you are? Come on, Que, you taught me the game. You had to know that before now."

"I have an idea, but I was never one hundred percent sure."

"Well, now you are. And knowing is half the battle."

"Yeah, aight, GI Joe, but let me ask you this: the Kia Optima I had when I killed Biggums, where is it?

"Good. So, let me ask you this: the Kia Optima I had when I killed Biggums, where is it?"

"You told me to get rid of it. I got rid of it."

"The Mercury Marauder we was in when I killed Landa?"

"Long gone, bruh. Set on fire the next day."

"The forty cal with the silencer attachment?"

"Bottom of the Anacostia River."

"The joints we killed Tommy with?"

"Serial numbers scraped off and sold to some niggas out in Virginia. The Acura we used that night been chopped up and the parts sold."

"I gave you the forty-five that I hit Mann with, what did you do with it?"

"That camo joint. 1911. You never even told me what you did with that joint, but I figured that it was fucked up, so I tossed it. Potomac River near Haynes Point."

"Smart. And I did tell you what I did with that joint. You just wasn't listening that day."

Jihad's phone vibrated. He turned the phone towards me. I could see Mike's number on the screen. I waved it off.

"I'll call him back in a minute." I stood up and stretched.

"The car that you put Mann in the trunk of, what about that joint?" Jihad asked. "Tabu said it was a Buick."

"It was. That was the car that Deucy took from the dude in the View. I had Lil Joe drive it to Ivanhoe Street and park it. I knew that I was gonna crush Mann, so I planned that whole move. I never touched it. The last person to touch the trunk was Mann right before I cooked him. Tabu shut the trunk, but he had on gloves. Whenever they find that nigga, that Buick can't be traced to me or Tab."

"What car did you push to get Mann to Ivanhoe Street?"

"The gold Nissan Armada that Tab used to push."

"That joint been gone. Salvaged for parts," Jihad informed.

"I used a stolen Toyota the night I crushed Diddy and Junie from the Cordas. I wiped it down and left it on K Street. Got rid of the guns that same night I bounced to Virginia Beach."

"Virginia Beach?"

"Yeah. Went there to chill with my author bitch Kiki Swinson. That's where I was when you buried Tabu."

"Is that right? You was out fuckin' while I was burying——"

I cut Jihad off before he could get started down a road that neither of us wanted to go down. "Don't start that shit, Jay. We talked about that at length, already. What happened to the Yukon we drove the night we crushed Cat Eye Dave at his mother's house?"

"It's out back in the parking lot."

"Get rid of it. The guns we used?"

"Traded away out Baltimore. Good man named Deli got 'em. He said he'll never tell anybody that he got them from Bo."

If You Cross Me Once 2

"A'ight. Good enough for me. One more thing, get rid of all your phones. As a matter of fact, get rid of everybody in the circle's phones. Take some money out the safe and buy all new phones. Personal and burners. I'ma toss mine later on and cop a new one in the morning."

"Got you, bruh. I'm on it. All new phones."

My phone and Jihad's phone both vibrated at the same time. He looked at his, then turned it around for me to see. "Tosheka."

I turned my phone around for Jihad to see. "Mike Carter."

We both smiled and said, "ignore" simultaneously, then pushed the buttons on our phones.

"Have you heard anything from Sean Branch lately?" Jihad asked.

"Naw. Not since we were last together. I'ma call him after I get a new phone. I wonder if he still got them two heads?!"

"I hope not. Because if he do, it's official. That nigga fucked up in the head. I mean like really fucked up. John Howard up St. Elizabeth, fucked up."

I walked to the kitchen and got juice out of the refrigerator. Opened a new jug and drank straight from it. I heard the apartment door open and shut. Then my phone vibrated again. I thought the caller was either Mike Carter or Tosheka, but it was Zin. I answered it. "Hey, baby, I was just thinking about you."

"Is that right? Well, I got a room at the Gaylord Hotel at the National Harbor. I'ma text you the info. See you when you get here."

"A'ight. I'm on my way."

When I ended the call, Jihad walked back through the door.

The smile on his face was a slick one. "Tosheka is still outside. She said she ain't leaving until you talk to her."

Shaking my head, I walked towards the balcony. I opened the balcony door.

"Where are you going?" Jihad asked.

"Duh? Off the balcony. We on the second floor. I can jump that. I'll holla at you tomorrow."

And with that said, I climbed down the balcony.

137

Anthony Fields

Chapter 17
SEAN BRANCH
Hope Village Halfway House

"This joint got six buildings. Forty, forty-four, fifty, and the three down the hill. One is the kitchen building. See right there where the security nigga in the burgundy shirt is standing?" Eric Ford asked.

I nodded my head. "I see him."

"Right there where he's standing is the cut that leads to the dining room and kitchen. There's so many niggas that come and go, the security nigga ain't gon' notice that you don't belong."

"Are you sure that Pig is in there? The dining room?"

Eric nodded. "He's in there. He go to breakfast about this time every weekday."

I looked out the window of the Dodge Charger painted Washington Redskins burgundy and saw dudes coming to and from on Longston Place in Southeast. I pulled the Department of Public Works hat down low. The hat matched the DPW jumper I had on with construction Timberland boots. The gun in my lap was brand new. I screwed on the sound muffler and put it in my jumper pocket. Then, without another word, I hopped out of the Charger and walked down Langston Place. There was a crowd of men on the way to the kitchen / dining room. I just fell in line with them. I walked past the security dude undetected.

Walking inside the building, I saw a line formed from up the stairs that ran down the stairs to where a female kitchen worker was passing out trays of food. I decided not to wait in line. I descended the stairs to the dining area. When I walked in, there were tables spread out all over the room. I spotted Pig sitting at a table eating. I whipped out the gun and beelined for him, covering the ground in seconds. Pig looked up and saw me coming, but he was stuck. I hit him in the face and his body fell forward. People scattered in all directions. I calmly shot Pig in the top of his head to make sure that he was dead. Then I ran out of the room, up the stairs, and out the building.

***

"You talked to Raf and Fice lately?"

"Naw. They haven't called me," Eric replied.

"Pull over up there by the building. I'ma have Taco come and scoop me, since you gotta go to work."

"Gotta keep the nine-to-five, slim. I'm tryna chill with——"

I pulled the muffled forty cal and blew Eric's brains all over the driver's side window. Using the jumper sleeve, I wiped down every surface in the Charger that I touched. Then I got out and started walking down South Capitol Street.

***

"Assalamu Alaikum. It's been a long time, Sean," Alex said as he came from around the counter to embrace me.

"Walaikum Assalam. Alex, my man, I'm just coming home and I need a good car to drive," I told him.

"I have a great car for you, Ocki. "What's your price range?"

"I don't have one. Tell me what you got?"

"Top of the line foreign whips. Mercedes C-class, E-class and S-class, BMW 645, 750 and 760's, Lexus 460's and 500's, Porsche——"

"Which Porsches do you have?"

"The one you need. The new 2013 911 GT coupe. You interested?"

"Very. Take me to them."

Alex led me to a section of cars that were gated off at the rear of the car lot. There were about twenty Porsches, all makes and models.

"What color do you like?"

"Champagne."

"That would be good," Alex said and walked me over to a Porsche 911. "This is the GT4 RS. Mid-engine, rear wheel drive, two-passenger, two-door hatchback. Carbon ceramic brakes, tan leather interior, Bose stereo system, satellite radio, Bluetooth inputs, eight speakers in door…"

I walked up to the Porsche and got inside. Leaning the driver's side seat back, I lost myself in the ambiance of the luxury sports car. "I want it."

"The tag on this baby is a little over a hundred——"

"I said I want it. Are you still the old Alex or are you on some 'new' Alex shit?"

"Sean, Ocki, times have changed, years have gone by, life has changed, but not me. I can do whatever you need me to do to put you behind the wheel of that Porsche. How much of a down payment——"

"No down payments. No car note. Paid in full. The whole hundred."

Alex smiled. "Come into my office and let's talk business. Have you had lunch yet? I can order Lebanese food from down the street. It's delicious." Alex looked towards the front of the dealership. "Do you have the money here with you now?"

"D.C. is thirty minutes away. I can go get it," I told Alex.

"Okay. We have been friends a long time. Leave me your driver's license here and take the Porsche. Consider it a test drive. Go get the money and I will do what I need to do to make everything official. I'll have the paperwork ready for you to sign upon your return."

"That's what's up."

Alex pulled out a cell phone and made a call. "Rashid, bring me the key fob for the gold 2013 Porsche 911 GT4 RS." He ended the call and turned back to me. "Time has preserved you well, Sean. And I love the beard."

***

"Where are you?!" Bolivia "Liv" Santos asked.

"I'm up Georgetown walking into Solbiato. Why? What's up?"

The buzzer on the door to the clothing store buzzed and the door opened. I walked inside the store with my eyes on all the shoes.

141

"No reason, bae. Just checking on you. Did you get the car?"

"Yeah, I got it."

"What kind of car?"

"A Porsche. The new 911."

"Okay, then, Mister 'I'm balling out of control'. Don't go to jail for speeding in that car. And don't kill yourself. You just got home. And I ain't finished giving you the 'Bolivia Experience', yet."

"The Bolivia Experience," I repeated. "Is that what you call it?"

"Uh huh," Liv said and laughed. "What are you doing when you leave there?"

"Meeting my daughter for lunch. Finally. She been ducking me."

"You know why."

"I do. But she gotta know it wasn't me," I lied. "I didn't kill her mother."

"I know you didn't. But you have to convince Shontay of that, not me."

"True dat. Hopefully, she'll listen."

"She will. Call me back later."

The connection ended. But before I could pocket the phone, another call came through. It was Quran. "Assalamu Alaikum, young'un. What's up?"

"You. Just wanted to check on you, big homie. How are you?"

"I'm good. About to do some shopping. Cop some new shit."

"Where you at?" Quran asked.

"Georgetown. In Solbiato's."

"A'ight. That's cool, but don't hit no other joint up there but the Hugo boss shop. After that, get the fuck from up there."

I laughed. "Damn, why you say that? What's wrong with Georgetown?"

"Big homie, ain't shit up there. You should've drove through there on your way to Mazza Galleria. They got the foreign clothes and shoes you need. Gucci, Prada, Balenciaga, Dior, Celine, Versace, Margielas, and all that big boy shit. If you stay in G-Town too long, you gon' be tempted to hit Prince's and Prances, then I'ma be

If You Cross Me Once 2

seeing your ass in some fat man Guess jeans, Morris Brown sweat suits, and throwback cream Filas and K-Swiss. And I can't let you go out like that. You been gone a long time. You still think Crystal's skating rink on Tuesday's is lady's night."

I cracked up laughing at Quran, partly because what he said was true. "A'ight, you got me, young'un. I'ma hit this joint and the Hugo Boss shop, and then I'ma scoop my daughter for lunch and head out to Tyson's."

"Good. You'll thank me later."

"A'ight. What's up with you, though?"

"Shit. On my way to hook up with Kiki. Still haven't talked to Mike yet, huh?"

"Naw. Haven't gotten around to it yet."

"He texted me five days ago and asked for your number. Did he call you?"

"Yeah, but I never responded. He called and I didn't answer."

"You gon' ever tell me what's up with the two of y'all?"

"Soon, Que, soon. Right now, I'm just focused on different shit. You heard about the nigga getting wiped down inside Hope Village this morning?"

"Of course. Shit been all over the news all day. The news said that the alleged shooter left the scene in a burgundy Dodge Charger. Then later they found a burgundy Dodge Charger blocks away with a man dead behind the wheel."

"Shit tragic, huh?"

"All the time."

"Muthafuckas gotta learn how to be more careful."

"I agree. I'ma get up with you later," Quran said.

"A'ight, young'un. Later."

"Can I help you with anything, my man?" a dude asked.

"Yeah, slim, let me get these." I pointed to one shoe, then several others. "These, these, these, and these, in an eight and a half."

Anthony Fields

If You Cross Me Once 2

Chapter 18
QURAN
Courtyard Hotel
Crystal City Virginia

"Damn, Que, you look good as shit," Kiki observed.

"Stop what you doing, Kiki. You look better."

Kiki stood by the couch in the room dressed in thigh high stockings attached to a garter on each leg. Her lace panties and bra matched the stockings and garters. Kiki had one child, a teenage son, but by looking at her body, you couldn't tell she had ever given birth. The polish on Kiki's fingers and toes also matched the red lingerie. It was a sexy sight.

"Whoever blessed you with them grey eyes and all that pretty hair should be celebrated."

"All that came from my father. His family genes."

"I'm assuming that that's where you got all that dick from then, too."

I walked over near Kiki and sat down on the couch. I untied each of my Nike Foamposite boots before I replied. "Definitely didn't get it from my mother."

"Stop playing, Que. You know what I meant."

I stood up and took my Hugo boss jeans off, then pulled the Boss sweatshirt over my head. I removed my tank top, but left my Hugo boxer briefs on. I grabbed Kiki and embraced her, kissed those big, luscious lips of hers.

Kiki grabbed my dick through the briefs. "What you been doing with this thing out here in these streets?"

I reached into Kiki's panties and massaged her clit, then stuck two fingers in her pussy. "What you been doing with this pussy out here in these streets?"

"I haven't been——"

I put my tongue in Kiki's mouth to silence her. She grinded her pussy on my fingers. I moved my lips around to her neck and licked her there. Then I freed her breasts from the lace bra. Visions of me sexing Zin all night long came to mind and I put them away. I wanted to focus on the job at hand. "How did you know that sexy lingerie turned me on?"

"Duh? You told me that the first time we was together."

"And you remembered?"

"I remembered. Que, you about to make me cum on your fingers."

"Cum for me, boo."

"I'm about to! I'm about to!"

Kiki's body shook and convulsed and she collapsed against me. I loved the way she orgasmed. It was almost violent the way she did it. I continued to piston my fingers in and out of her while simultaneously licking her ears and neck.

"Que...Que," Kiki moaned as she held me tight.

"Cum one more time before I put my tongue in you."

"Whooo - oo - Que! I need that dick in me!"

"Not until you cum on my finger again."

"Qu - e - e - eee!"

"Cum for me!" I demanded.

True to her freaky nature, Kiki moved as if she was being electrocuted. Her moans got loud and pierced the ceiling, then loudly, she climaxed again. I scooped Kiki into my arms and carried her to the bed. I laid her down and removed her panties. Kiki's legs opened wide. I dived in between her legs and lapped at her soaking wet pussy as if it was dessert. Her hands gripped my head and pushed my head into her middle. I used my nose, lips, and chin to massage Kiki's clit.

"Que, please… Put…your…dick…in…me!"

Kiki rose up off her back and pushed me up. She pushed me backwards and grabbed at my briefs. She pulled them down my legs and off. Then she leaped at my dick and engulfed it in her mouth. Kiki sucked me vigorously for minutes before she got up and positioned herself over me. She guided me to her pussy and sat down. Once completely filled, Kiki rode me like a wild woman. Her pussy was so warm, wet, and tight that I couldn't hold back my nut for long.

"Damn, boo, this pussy torch! I'm about to cum!"

If You Cross Me Once 2

Me saying that must've touched a button inside Kiki. She gyrated herself up and down, to and fro, back and forth, side to side. When I finally let go inside her, I was lightheaded, exhausted. Drained.

"Gotdamn!" was all I could say over and over again.

***

I fell asleep without knowing it and was awakened by the sounds of a vibrating phone. I reached out as if mine was nearby, but it wasn't. It was in my pants pocket over by the couch. The curtains inside the hotel room were drawn shut, so the room was semi-dark. Light from Kiki's phone illuminated. Kiki was knocked out asleep. I rose up and looked over her body to the phone on the table by the bed.

The name "Juice" appeared on her phone's screen as it vibrated over and over again. I smiled to myself, remembering what Sean Branch had said to me…

"… never said anything about it, but I was in the joint with her husband. Good bamma named Julien Seay. They call him Juice. All that nigga talk about is that bitch. She's his claim to fame."

A wicked thought crossed my mind. Quickly, I got off the bed on my side and walked around to the other side of the bed. As I got there, the phone call ended. I stood by the table by the bed.

"Call back, nigga," I whispered. "Call back."

Then as if head heard me, the dude Juice called Kiki's phone back. I picked up the phone and swiped right to answer the call.

"This call is from a federal prison. This is a prepaid call. You will not be charged for this call. This call is from - (Juice). To accept this call, press five, now…"

I pressed the five and laid the phone back on the table. Then I took my dick and forced it into Kiki's mouth. She awoke and accepted my dick.

"Damn, Kiki! Suck that dick! Suck it!"

Still laid on her side, Kiki grabbed my dick and ate it loudly. Her moans of pleasure made my dick harder. I grabbed her face and forced my dick deeper into her mouth until she gagged.

I glanced at the phone and saw that the timer was still going, which indicated that the call hadn't ended. The caller hadn't said a word that I could hear. I pulled my dick from Kiki's mouth and told her, "Get up on your knees. All fours."

Kiki complied and never thought to look in the table's direction. I slid in behind her phat ass and put my dick in her. She still wore the garters and stockings. Reaching down, I gripped both of Kiki's ankles and pounded myself into her body.

"O - o - o - h - h…s - s - h - h - i - t - t!"

"Damn this pussy good, Kiki!"

"O - oh, shit! Fuck me, Que! Fuck this pussy!"

"Who pussy is this? Huh? Whose is it?!"

"This is your pussy, Que! It's your pussy!"

I thought about the man on the other end of the phone and imagined him with tears in his eyes. "Can I fuck you in your ass? Cum all in that ass?!"

"Yes! Yes, Que! Please fuck my ass!"

I glanced at the phone. The call was still going. Her husband hadn't hung up yet. I pulled my dick out of Kiki's wet pussy and put it in her accepting back door, inch by inch until I was all the way inside her.

"O - o - w - w, Que! You… hurting… me! You…hurting…my…ass!"

Grinding slowly into Kiki, I gripped her hips and smiled.

"Who's ass is this?"

"It's yours, Que!"

"Can I cum in your ass?"

"Yes, please!"

Glancing at the phone one more time, I pounded Kiki's ass until I exploded.

If You Cross Me Once 2

Chapter 19
BLAST

The 2600 block of Langston Place was home to one of the most notorious projects that D.C. ever had. There were four buildings that made up Langston Lane. All four buildings were painted different colors on their facades. There were people in front of every building when I pulled my Lexus onto the Lane. I spotted Doo Doo in front of the second building, involved in a crap game. I parked and got out of the car. I walked up to the game. All eyes fell on me as I approached. Hands went to waistbands.

Doo Doo looked up and saw one standing near him. "Ease up. He's with me." To me, Doo Doo said, "Gimme a minute, Blast, I'ma break theses niggas, then holla at you."

I nodded my head and waited patiently for Doo Doo to finish gambling.

***

"I'm sorry about our brother, bob. Him and Whistle were my men."

The look on Doo Doo's face was disingenuous. He leaned on a brand new Cadillac CTS-V wagon. I spotted the paper tags.

"I already know that, bruh. I'm fucked up about big bruh, but I know that he was into a rack of wild shit. Look, slim, I'ma cut to the chase. I'm trying to pay for my brother's funeral and all that, and I'm short on cash. I need a lick. Fuck with me."

Doo Doo pulled out a pack of Newport cigarettes, extracted one, and lit up. "I feel you on what you need to do, but I ain't got no lick for you right now. Gimme a few days."

"Have you ever tasted the food from that new spot on Half Street called Wings and Things?"

"Naw. Never even heard of it. What's up with the food?"

"Let's hit that joint and talk, slim. If you can't help me, I might can help you."

"Is that right?" Doo asked.

"Ride with me to the food spot, hear me out, and you decide if you like my offer."

"A'ight, bet. My car or yours?"

"Mine. I'll have you back here in a little while."

Doo Doo followed me to my Lexus. He got inside at the same moment I did. I made up some shit to talk to Doo Doo about as I drove through the city to my destination. I turned off of M Street onto Half Street in Southwest, D.C.

Half Street was lined on both sides with private homes and project tenements until it reached an area that was under heavy construction. I pulled the Lexus behind Ren's Infiniti truck and parked.

"I need to pit stop for a minute, slim," I told Doo Doo.

His eyes scanned the deserted area. Panic set in. Doo Doo reached for his waist, but I was quicker on the draw. I pulled my gun and pointed at him.

"Damn, slim," Doo Doo said. "What's up with you?"

Before I could respond, Ren walked up to the car and pulled open the passenger door of the Lexus, a gun in hand. I got out of the car and walked around to the sidewalk. "Get out the car, Doo Doo. We need to talk."

"This is crazy, Blast. You didn't have to do all this geekin'-ass shit. We could've talked anywhere. What's up, though?" Doo Doo replied as he got out of the car, but leaned on it. "You and baby girl out here with hammers out on a nigga. Fuck is up?"

I put the gun up and stood in front of Doo Doo. Ren stood next to me. "Last Friday, somebody killed my brother and your man Whistle in a house on Third Street. Word on the street is that you was there. Is that true, slim?"

Doo Doo started to shake his head.

I spoke quickly. "Bruh, if you start lying to me, I'ma kill you out here. Believe that. So, let me ask you again, was you in that house on Third when my brother got killed?"

Resignation crossed Doo Doo's face mixed with defeat. "I was there."

"Your phone number was in my brother's call log of his cell phone. You and Whistle were the last people that he spoke to. How do I know? Because Crud was on my mother's plan and she gets all of the texts and calls. She pulled up the data. I saw all the text messages that you and Whistle sent Crud. Y'all pressed him out to come to the house on Third Street. Why? To kill him? Did you and Whistle kill Crud?"

"Fuck naw. Crud was my man."

"Tell me why y'all wanted him to come to that house."

"Somebody wanted to talk to him. Asked us to get him there. To talk. I swear to you, slim, I had no idea that they wanted to kill him."

"Who is 'they', slim? Who asked you to get my brother to Third Street?"

"He gon' kill me if I tell you."

I pulled the gun back out and chambered around for dramatic effect. "I'm gonna kill you if you don't talk."

"It was Sean Branch and his man Quran," Doo Doo confessed.

"Sean Branch and Quran? Who the fuck are they?" I asked.

"Quran I heard of, but don't really know. Sean Branch, I was in the feds with. He's a vicious nigga. Just came home a few weeks ago. While we was in Florence, we was cellies for a little while. I showed him my photos and told him about my friends.

"I told him about Whistle. Whistle had sent me flicks of him and Crud and other niggas. He wrote all the niggas names on the back of the pictures. So I knew who Crud was, but I never met him until I came home. When I came home, Whistle brought Crud to the halfway with him when he dropped off some clothes and money. So when Sean called me and said that he needed to talk to Crud and he needed me to set up the meet, I agreed."

"Sean Branch," I repeated, wondering where I'd heard the name before.

Doo Doo continued, "Whistle was with me. I told him to remind Crud to come to the house, but like I said earlier, I never knew what Sean wanted to talk about or that he was gonna kill anybody."

"We never found my brother's car. Where is it?"

"I don't have a clue. I never asked Crud how he got to the house. He never said. I never asked. Neither did Whistle. Never looked out the window and saw how he got there. Crud called Whistle and said he was about to knock on the door. Whistle opened it and let him in."

"Then what?" I asked.

"About an hour later, Sean and his man showed up. He said something about Crud told on his man, Lacy. Said he promised his man that he was gon' kill Crud when he got home. He made good on the promise. I tried to tell him to chill, but he wouldn't listen. He pulled out a big-ass knife and stabbed Crud in the neck."

"What was Crud doing when Sean stabbed him?"

"Nothing. He folded up and Sean went crazy. He cut Crud's head off in front of us. Then he shot the body up before taking the head with him. His man Quran killed Whistle."

"Why? Because he was a witness? If so, how did you survive?"

"The dude Quran killed Whistle because they said Whistle told on them MLK Avenue dudes, too. Not because he was a witness to Crud's murder."

"Doo Doo, what happened before Sean killed my brother? Something else happened. What was it?"

Doo Doo got antsy and started to look scared. His lip quivered a little as he spoke. "Nothing happened. Sean walked in, said what he said, and then stabbed Crud in the neck. He cut his head off, put it in a bag with the knife, and left."

"You're lying to me, Doo Doo. Baby, shoot him for me."

Ren shot Doo Doo in the leg. He grabbed at the hole in his leg.

"Fuck you do that for? I'm telling you the truth about what happened."

"Start from the beginning and tell me everything that happened, again."

Doo Doo retold his whole story about what happened at the house on Third Street the day my brother was killed. But still he lied.

"Let me tell you something, slim. The detective on the case told my mother… Who set the house on fire?"

"They did."

"You're lying, slim. You just told your side of the story twice and never once did you mention Sean Branch and the dude Quran setting the house on fire."

"O-o-o-w-w, my leg fucked up. I'm bleeding to death! I'm getting weak."

"In a minute, more than your leg gon' be fucked up, if you don't stop lying to me. My mother talked to the detectives. They told her that my brother was found tied up. He was bound, slim. Your story never mentions Crud getting tied up by anyone. So, how did my brother get tied up? How did he get hogtied? Who tied him up? It had to be either you or Whistle. Who did it?"

"Whistle did," Doo Doo said, defeated. "Whistle tied Crud up."

"Whistle did it? By himself? How the fuck Whistle gon' tie Crud up by himself? Crud was bigger than Whistle. And when he do it? Before or after Sean and Quran got there?"

"Before."

"But why would he do that, if the both of y'all thought Sean Branch just wanted to talk to Crud?"

Doo Doo didn't respond. He just stared at the blood on his pants.

"Cat got your tongue, huh? I'ma tell you what happened. Sean Branch is a friend of yours from the feds. He remembers that you know Crud and Whistle. Sean wants to kill Crud for him allegedly snitching on his man, Lacy. He pays you to set it up. You brought in Whistle, probably paid him. Had to pay him to go against Crud. You and Whistle convince Crud to come to the house on Third Street. Crud doesn't suspect anything. He believes that you and Whistle are his men. Crud comes through. You and Whistle ambush him and tie him up. Sean and Quran came through. Then things happen like you said from there. Sean Branch kills Crud and cuts off his head. Quran kills Whistle. They pay you, and then you try to set the house on fire to cover up the crime. Admit it, Doo Doo. You was with that plot, wasn't you?"

Doo Doo's eyes filled with tears. He shook his head.

"It's true. Everything I just said is what happened. It's cool, though. You can still save yourself, Doo Doo. Tell me everything you know about Sean Branch. The dude Quran killed Whistle. I'm not concerned about that. But Sean gotta pay for killing my brother."

"He'll kill me if I talk. Worse than any death you can give me."

"Cool. Have it your way, then. Ren, Doo Doo wants to die. Give him his wish."

Ren shot Doo Doo in his face. Once his body dropped, she shot him some more. I rifled through Doo Doo's pockets, taking his money and cell phone. It was a Tracfone burner flip phone. I scrolled through the contacts until I saw a number for Sean Branch. Smiling, I sent him a text.

Chapter 20
ZIN
CENTRAL DETENTION FACILITY (D.C. JAIL)

"Excuse me, ma'am," I said, knocking on the plexiglass of the booth called a "bubble", where the female CO sat. "I asked to see two inmates, Anthony Williams and David Battle, over an hour ago. Can you tell me what the hold-up is?"

"The supervisor said that the count has to clear before we can permit inmate movement through the facility, Ms. Carter. As soon as the count clears, the inmates will be brought in shortly thereafter," the CO replied.

"Thank you."

I went back to the small legal visiting room and read over the file for Anthony Williams. His entire case was based on grainy video footage of a man in a red Honda pulling into a parking space in front of Holiday Liquors, a liquor store in a tiny strip mall off of Wheeler Road in Southeast, D.C. The car parked and a lone man got out and opened fire on a man who has just exited the liquor store. After the victim fell, the man stood over the victims and shot him four more times. Then the man ran back to the Honda and pulled out of the parking lot. That was the first murder.

The second murder happened ten minutes later on Mississippi Avenue near the Trenton Park housing complex. The same Honda from the Holiday Liquors murder was recorded turning into the complex. A man - the same man - got out of the Honda and ran towards three men in front of a school. The man opened fire on all three men, injuring one and killing one. Then he ran away. Law enforcement recovered the red Honda where it was parked last days later. There were several latent fingerprints pulled from all over the Honda, several that matched Anthony Williams.

I heard the sound of the visiting hall's sliding metal door and looked up to see several inmates entering the visiting area. Other attorneys waited in rooms just like mine for their clients. I spotted both of mine. I recognized Anthony Williams from the photos in the file. I got up and met David Battle and Anthony Williams.

"Our interview will take longer, Mr. Williams. Let me talk to David first, then I'll come and get you."

"A'ight," Anthony Williams said and sat on the bench near the receivers attached to the plexiglass made for social visits.

"Hey, Ms. Carter," David Battle said and followed me to the room.

Once we were seated and the door was closed, I said, "Hey, David. Good news and bad news. Which one do you want first?"

"Doesn't matter. Talk to me."

"Okay. The good news is that I talked to Heather Pinckney and the clerk of the courts. I was able to have Heather withdrawn from your case and to enter my appearance as your lawyer on the gun charge. Quran insisted that I do it and he paid all of your legal fees. The two of you must be really close."

"That's my sandbox homie. We grew up together."

"I got everything pertaining to your case from Heather this morning and it's exactly what I said it was. A charge that can stick because of the traffic violation."

"Wasn't no traffic violation. They lied. The arresting officer knew me from the neighborhood. They probably heard about my name being mentioned in the Solomon Robinson murder and wanted to fuck with me. I wasn't speeding through no parking lot. I signaled, turned into the red brick parking lot, and parked. Simple as that. If that's the bad news, I knew all of that already."

"Uh…no, that's not the bad news. The bad news is that Greg Gamble is doing exactly what I said he would. Ian McNealy isn't offering you any type of plea deal besides you cooperating."

"Cooperating? He can suck my——"

"Hey! Maintain your composure. We know that that ain't gonna happen, so I paid those emails no mind. But that's how the game is gonna be played. I told you, it's not Ian McNealy; it's Greg Gamble. He's mad because we beat him in that hearing. He hates me."

"You? If he hates you, then maybe it wasn't a good idea for you to take my case," David said casually.

"Well, I can always refund Quran his money and withdraw from the case. You can find somebody that Greg Gamble doesn't hate."

"Naw, I'm good. I'm sorry, Ms. Carter, just a little irritated, that's all. I don't want another lawyer on my case."

"Good. And I accept your apology. Besides, Greg Gamble is going to hate anyone that appears as your lawyer. He hates you, too. It's the goody two shoes syndrome, or maybe even a God complex. Who knows? I'm still gonna do everything in my power to get you a cop to time served."

"Thanks, Ms. Carter, for everything. Especially coming to see Antbone."

"You asked; I checked his file. I think his case is beatable. Let me talk to him and see what type of vibe I get from him. Then I'll decide whether or not to take his case. If I take it, it won't be pro bono. Quran is paying your legal fees. Do you have the money to pay his?"

"Price range?" David asked.

"Double homicide. Twenty and twenty. Forty grand."

David rose from his seat. "Deal. Go and talk to shorty and let me know what you decide. Then I'll get a retainer fee to you."

"Sounds good to me."

"I'ma go ahead and bounce. Get at me if you hear anything."

"I will. And please send Mr. Williams in here."

***

Jonathan Zucker was one of the best criminal defense attorneys in the greater Washington area. He sat across from me at his desk on the phone. He put up one finger to signal to me that he'd be only a minute. I looked around his office and noticed all the awards that Jon Zucker had won. He had commendations aplenty and even a key to a city. The city was called Kenosha and was somewhere in

Wisconsin. Jon's law degree from Brown was on display along with his bar certification.

"Zin," Jon Zucker said after ending his call. "Talked to your dad and he's excited about where we're going with this. I also talked to Maryann Settles. This whole affidavit thing is the real deal. She's all the way on board the 'Free Michael Carter' ship. I'm sending my investigator to interview her on Friday when she's free. She'll be deposed. Her husband, too. I've already worked on the newly discovered evidence motion. Actually, I'm filing motions under three different sections. I'm doing a Rule 33 motion, a 23-110 post-conviction litigation motion, and an 'Actual Innocence' motion. Asking for an immediate evidentiary hearing in each."

"Good strategy, Jon. I like it."

"I thought you would."

"You do know that we are getting ready to fight the fight of our lives, don't you?"

"How so?" Jon Zucker asked.

"Greg Gamble is going to call in all of his markers, favors, and political connections. I just beat him in the Sean Branch retrial. I beat him in court for my client David Battle. Greg Gamble is not going to go away easily. He's not going to lie down and take this beating on the chin. This is the beginning of round one. I'm just saying, strap in and get ready for a full twelve round fight. And a rematch if he loses."

"I love a good fight, Zin. Twelve rounds or two, I'm ready."

"That's a good attitude to have. You're gonna need it."

Chapter 21
SEAN BRANCH

"Baby, I need you to go out to the garage and check and see if there's a dead animal trapped in there somewhere, because something in there stinks like hell. Smells like roadkill or some bad park."

"I got you, Liv," I said and smiled. I know exactly what the smell was: the two heads that had been decomposing in the trash bag I'd put them in a week ago. They'd been in Liv's garage ever since. I got up off the couch and walked up behind Liv as she took groceries out of a Safeway bag in the kitchen. I wrapped my arms around her waist and kissed her neck.

"Stop, Sean. You know my neck is the jackpot spot," Liv moaned.

"I love hitting the jackpot," I replied.

Liv tried to wiggle out of my embrace, but I didn't let her. "Stop, before we start fucking, and I need to eat first. You must've popped one of them Mojo pills or something, with your horny ass. Starting shit in the middle of the day like this."

I laughed at Liv. "Mojo pill? Fuck I'ma get one of them from?"

"The gas station where everybody else gets theirs from?"

"I don't know what them niggas you was fucking with before me was on, but I ain't gotta pop no pills," I informed Liv and lifted her skirt.

"Sean, stop!" Liv protested. "Ain't that your phone vibrating?"

"Fuck that phone."

Liv gave in to the seduction. She stepped out of her heels and wiggled her butt against my middle. "Fuck the phone or fuck me?"

I pulled Liv's panties down to her ankles. "I'd rather fuck you."

"Handle your business then, brotha."

Bending Liv over on the kitchen counter, I did what she requested. I handled my business.

***

I pulled up to the corner of Alabama Avenue and Naylor Road and looked out for the car that Doo Doo said he was in. According to him, he had some important info that he needed to give me in person. I read all of his text messages again. Then something inside me felt off. I pulled onto Naylor Road near Altimont Street. I read the text message again for the fourth time, trying to figure out why I had the funny feeling I had. As I looked up, I saw a beautiful woman with red hair and a dude exit a Lexus LS 460. I looked around again for Doo Doo. I glanced at the time on the phone. He was late. I looked at the text messages again, then at the couple approaching my car. They were moving funny to me, but I dismissed my concern as paranoia. I glanced back at the text messages on the phone, then like a sudden epiphany, it hit me. Doo Doo could barely read or write. Whoever had sent the text messages wrote out every word correctly.

Just as I looked up, I saw both man and woman pulling guns. My brain screamed "hit", and I reacted. I ducked low as the gunshots rang out. I hit the gas on the Porsche and pulled off quickly. My back window blew out. I could hear the bullets hitting the car as I got out of Dodge. I drove away angry that someone had just tried to kill me, a man and a woman that I had never seen before in my life. I seared the silver Lexus LS 460 into my head, racked my brain trying to think of anyone I knew who drove a car like that. I couldn't think of anyone - at least not anyone connected to Doo Doo.

Pulling over suddenly, I did the whole body check thing to ensure that I hadn't been shot and didn't know it. After that, I surveyed the Porsche. I saw all of the bullet holes in the car. I saw all the shattered glass in the back seat and floor. I smiled despite my anger. All I could think about was killing Doo Doo and the couple who'd just tried to ambush me. Had I never realized the correct spelling in the text messages that came from Doo Doo's phone, I'd be dead. I walked all around the Porsche. My blood boiled just thinking about the brazen daylight attempt on my life, but still I smiled and laughed. I added three more people to my list of the walking dead.

If You Cross Me Once 2

May Allah have mercy on their souls when I caught them. The first one being Doo Doo.

Anthony Fields

Chapter 22
QURAN
1351 Howard Road
Southeast D.C.

"What happened with Tosheka yesterday after I left? Did she stay outside? I asked Jihad as I rolled up a blunt of OG Kush.

"I went outside and told her that you was gone. I guess she decided that if she couldn't beat us, she might as well join us," Jihad replied and smiled.

"Join us? Fuck your talkin' about, Jay?"

"What I mean is that it must've dawned on her that she couldn't have what she wanted: you. So, she settled for the next best thing. Me. We went up to the MLK Deli and got some food. Stopped on Talbert, copped some weed and Patron, and it was on. I fucked her all last night until the sun came up."

"As you should've. But be careful with her, bruh. No pillow talking."

"I already know that, big bruh. What happened with Kiki earlier that you said you had to tell me?"

I explained to Jihad what I'd done to Kiki and how I accepted the jail call and let her husband listen to me fuck her.

Jihad laughed. "Damn, bruh. You are a heartless muthafucka. I thought you fucked with Kiki. Why you do her like that?"

"To be honest with you, Jay, I don't even know. It wasn't planned. Sean told me that he was in the joint with a dude that was married to Kiki. Told me the dude's name was Juice. I dismissed it because I figured that Kiki would've said something about being married. All the time I been fucking with her, I never thought nothing about who else she was fuckin' or if she had a dude until Sean put that husband shit in my head. So earlier, when I saw her phone ringing on vibrate and the name Juice kept popping up, I just got on some wild shit and answered the call. I guess it's better that he knows what his wife is on out here. And it just goes to prove that you can't trust these bitches out here. They can live double and triple lives. They are the best liars. The best cheaters. The best planners."

"The Quran says that Allah is the best of planners," Jihad interjected.

"True dat, but you know what I mean. You get what I'm tryna say. These broads out here is vicious."

"Like Tosheka, huh?"

"Point made."

"Well, what about Zin?"

"What about her?"

"Does she fall in these categories too? Can she be trusted?"

"Baby boy, I really believe that Zin is different. Can I trust her? Yes. She knows that I killed Tab and Landa, Tommy, and others. She's still here, and the decision to let her in on all of that hasn't come back to haunt me yet. She was raised well by a father who taught me the game. I think Zin is the exception to the rule."

"I sure hope so, bruh. For your sake and mine. And speaking of her father, Mike is about to call us in a few. He just texted me."

***

"The vacation is over, Que. Y'all ready to get back to work?" Mike Carter asked.

"Always. What you get for us, big guy?" I replied.

"Two jobs, actually. Three targets. Money paid through the usual channels."

"A'ight. Tell me what the jobs are."

"The first job is Joseph 'JoJo' Morris. Vicious, cheese-eating rat. He jumped on a lot of good men's cases and testified against them. But this one is for a good Baltimore man named Gutta. Came in on a blood conspiracy. Murdaland Mafia Piru or some shit like that. While at the fed holdover spot out Baltimore, JoJo befriended Gutta, impersonated a real nigga, and Gutta went for it. All the time, JoJo was conspiring to cook Gutta for the government, which he ended up doing, and now he's home. He's from Sursum Corda."

If You Cross Me Once 2

"Another one of them niggas? The Cordas might got the record for having the wickedest collection of niggas in any one neighborhood in the city. Damn!" Jihad commented.

"Damn, young'un, I never thought about it like that," Mike said, "but you right. And that's crazy because the second job is another vicious rat named Eric, but they call him Baby E. He's from Clay Terrace. He's got all the weed, I'm hearing. Got a Cali connect. Anyway, he's fronting a rack of weed to a bitch named KD who lives out where?"

"Let me guess." I chimed in. "Sursum Cordas."

"Ding, ding, ding. If this was a game, you'd get the prize. But unfortunately, this shit ain't a game," Mike emphasized. "And the two of you know the universal law."

"A rat anywhere is a threat to the good men everywhere," me and Jihad said in unison.

"Correct. The bitch told on some good men, Bernard 'Tadpole' Johnson and some other dudes on that 'L' Street conspiracy back in the day. Her government name is Kendra Dyson…"

***

Riding down North Capital Street in my tinted Cadillac XTS, I looked around for either JoJo Morris or KD. "Let me see that picture of the hot bitch again."

Jihad passed me his phone. I studied the faces of both targets again.

"How do you think Mike got the picture of KD?"

I shrugged my shoulders. "Hot bitch been out here getting to a bag for a minute, I hear. She ain't hiding. Bitch going out to clubs and parties hanging around niggas like she's official. Don't surprise me that there's pictures of her floating around. Now, if Mike had a picture of Joe Morris, then I'd be surprised."

"I'm hip, huh? Well, what about Baby E? How are we gonna get to him?"

"Baby E gon' be easy to get, baby boy. I made some calls already. Niggas claim they ain't never seen no paperwork on him and he's feeding the hood, so he's comfortable. He doesn't think nobody

165

will come into Clay Terrace and get him. We gon' prove him wrong. To me, I think JoJo Morris is gonna be the hardest to get. He's more mobile. Has too many hoods to hang out in. He busts his gun and gets money, so he gon' cater to the young niggas that are too young to know or care if he hot or not. He hangs out on 15th Place in Congress Park, in the Cordas, and he hangs Uptown near Kennedy Street. Nobody can pin him down to one spot."

"Don't matter. We gon' get him. I'ma pin his ass to the pavement when we do."

"Aye, let me ask you something. Earlier, you said that Sursum Cordas got the most rats in one hood than any other hood. How many the Cordas got?"

"What? You don't know?" Jihad said. "The nigga Moe Cheeks was a vicious killer rat. He dead now, but he was hot as shit. The nigga Freddy 'Lee Lee' Bailey, Calvin that they called Moose, hot as shit, and I'm hearing that he was some kin to JoJo Morris. He dead, too, but was a wicked nigga. Nitty that went in on that li'l girl Princess' murder made statements on them Barry Farms niggas the Cordas was beefing with in the early two thousands. You killed Diddy and Junie, both rats, both from the Cordas. Corey Ryland—"

"The jury is out still deliberating on him."

"A'ight. I give you that. It was never confirmed on him, but niggas still got his name in their mouths as one of them."

"Niggas will say anything. You know that. Who else?"

"The light-skinned nigga Ed with the long hair. I was over the jail with him years ago. Don't remember his last name, but there was paperwork all over the jail about him. The wild nigga G-Rob, and now Kendra and JoJo. What about the old head nigga Kenny Man?"

"Kenneth Bryant. Put major work in back in the day. I heard some wild shit, but ain't nobody ever confirmed nothing on him. He's out in the feds running shit in an FCI, I heard. That's crazy, though. One neighborhood done breed so many wicked muthafuckas."

"It's the way of the world now, big bruh. The way of the world."

If You Cross Me Once 2

***

The Mid Atlantic seafood spot on St. Barnabas Road was packed with people. I grabbed the bag with my food in it and Jihad did the same. When we exited it, I opened the door of the Cadillac and set the food down. Jihad opened his bag and extracted a Styrofoam tray filled with fried fish, grilled Brussel sprouts, and rice and gravy. He set the tray down in the hood of the car.

Sean was dressed in all black attire. His hair was cut and perfectly trimmed. His beard looked to be oiled up. I met him in the parking lot and embraced him. I could feel the gun on his waist.

"Assalamu Alaikum."

"Walaikum Assalam. Sean, what's good, slim?"

"I'm good, Que. By the mercy of Allah. Somebody tried to kill me today." Sean then went on to explain to me everything that happened.

"Hold on, big homie. Before I comment, let me introduce you to my brother, Jihad." I called Jay over. "Jay, this is Sean Branch. Sean, my brother, Jihad."

"What's up, big bruh?" Jihad said. He wiped his hand on a napkin and walked over to greet Sean. He held out his hand.

Sean swiped at Jihad's hand and moved in for an embrace. Once it was broken, he said, "Your father was like a father to me. Quran is my brother, and that makes you my brother, too. Last time I saw you, you were young as shit. I heard a lot of good things about you, young'un. Your pops would be proud."

Jihad smiled. "Thanks, bruh. Heard a lot about you, too. Too many stories for me to count them all. My brother is your biggest fan——"

"Fuck you mean, fan, nigga!" I said loudly.

"Don't kill me, big bruh, I was just kidding. But on some real shit, it's good to finally meet you, bruh. You're a whole legend in these streets."

"Cut that shit out, young'un. But, check this out. I gotta find out who that broad and dude was that sparked at me. So, I gotta find this nigga Doo Doo."

"You should have let me kill him that night on Third Street," I told Sean.

"I already know. I fucked up, and now I was almost killed. Won't happen again. Ever. I'ma find Doo Doo and roast his ass, then I'ma find that bitch and the nigga with her and do the same thing to them. Then I can resume settling all my old beefs."

"What did you do with them heads?"

"Had to get rid of 'em, even though I didn't want to. They had the garage smelling like rotten meat, ass, and feet. When I kill Doo Doo n'em, I'ma take their heads, too."

Jihad looked at me. "This nigga lunching like shit. I thought you was bad, but bruh got even you beat."

"You gotta be vicious to get a head, young'un," Sean said and smiled. "Get it?"

I saw the way Jay looked at Sean, and all I could do was laugh.

If You Cross Me Once 2

Chapter 23
BLAST

"The murder rate in the city continues to rise. Metropolitan police were called to the scenes of four separate shootings today where five people died. The first shooting occurred in the 1800 block of Savannah Street in Southeast. Three people were shot in front of a building. Witnesses say that two masked men walked up to a crowd of men standing in front of 1891 Savannah. Both men pulled guns and opened fire. Two of the three men who were shot were pronounced dead at the scene. A third man is at a local hospital fighting for his life.

"Two hours later, a man was shot as he exited a vehicle in the 3600 block of Jay Street in Northeast. He later died at a nearby hospital.

"Thirty minutes later, authorities were called to 48th and Sheriff Road about a domestic dispute. Police arrived to find a woman identified as Loretta Dunn suffering from multiple stab wounds to her neck, face, and chest. She later died while being transported to a hospital.

"A man on his way home from work discovered a person who'd been shot on the unit block of Half Street in Southwest near Audi field this evening. The man was pronounced dead on the scene. Authorities identified the man as 31-year-old James Yarborough——"

I clicked the TV off and stared down at the back of Ren's head as it bobbed up and down on my lap. I tried to give in to the pleasure that getting head gave me, but I couldn't. My thoughts were elsewhere. I couldn't believe that Sean Branch had gotten away after the perfect ambush.

Ren stopped what she was doing and looked up at me, slob on her chin, spit pooled on her fist. "I was trying to take your mind off of Naylor Road, but I can see that you're still distracted."

"I'm sorry, baby. But you're right. I am. How in the fuck did he anticipate what we were about to do? It's as if he saw it coming. Knew it was coming. The way he looked at us and then pulled off before we could finish him. That shit still has me baffled. I mean…he was right there. I knew it was him from the description Doo Doo gave us. Light-skinned, black haircut low, a big beard… It was him. How did he see the hit coming? Shit has my head all fucked up."

Ren got up off knees. She smiled as she pulled her shirt over her head. Next, she removed her bra. Her eyes never left mine as she slid out of her jeans and panties. Ren climbed on top of me. "Don't sweat it, baby. We gon' get him. It just wasn't his time to die. But Sean Branch is going to get exactly what's coming to him. We found him once; we'll find him again. And the next time will be his last. Now, can I get what's coming to me?"

My dick stiffened as Ren grabbed it. She sat on my lap and moved her wet pussy all around it, moaning all the while. Slowly, I forgot about Sean Branch. Ren lifted up and sat down on my erection. She gyrated and winded all over me. Suddenly, we were the only two people in the world.

***

I pulled into a parking spot on my mother's street and got out of the car. I used my key to get into the family home. It was late, but I knew that Bionca would be up. I was right. Bionca was seated at the dining room table, her laptop in front of her.

She looked up at me as I approached. "You're up late. As usual." Bionca went back to what she was doing on the laptop.

"You know me. Last to sleep, first one to rise. What brings you here this late?"

I grabbed a chair and moved it close to my sister. I saw that she was assembling pictures of Crud and the family together in a collage.

"For the memorial. There will be a large poster like picture of Byron sitting on a…whatever that thing is called. There will be obituaries with photos. A lot of photos. A couple people will speak. Mommy, of course; me, Brechelle, you if you want to, other family and friends. There will be a few songs sung, some poems read. That's about it. Then we'll find a place for a repast. Mommy hasn't picked a date yet for the memorial, but Byron's being cremated at a crematorium out in Brandywine, MD next week. So, again, what brings you here this late?"

I told Bionca everything that I'd learned and everything that had happened since we had last spoke.

"Sean Branch, huh?" Bionca said, her facial expression unreadable.

"Yeah," I replied. "You hip to him?"

Bionca rose from her seat and walked over by the kitchen's entrance. She paced the floor there before coming back towards me. "I'm hip to Sean Branch, Brion. And damn near the whole D.C. is hip to him. He's bad news. Dangerous. Vicious. Just came home about a month ago, I think. I saw it all over the news. Back in the day, he killed so many people and got away with it that the streets nicknamed him Teflon Sean. No murder charges were ever brought up on him. No crime could stick to him. But he ending up getting charged for a murder that he didn't commit, and somehow, he got found guilty of it. That was over eighteen years ago. He's got to be like thirty-nine or forty. Looks like a Hispanic person with dark curly hair."

"That's him. He's grown a beard now."

"The game just got super serious, baby brother. You tried to kill Sean Branch, and didn't you said he looked at you?"

"Yeah, he looked right at me and Ren, then he ducked low and got out of there. We put over twenty rounds or better in his car. A Porsche with paper tags on it. Still can't figure out how he figured out that we was gonna hit him."

"Sean Branch is a different kind of killer. He's been rumored to have been killing since he was like eleven or twelve. Maybe younger. He saw your face, so he knows what you look like - not who you are, but what you look like, and that ain't good. Now, it all makes sense. Cutting off Byron's head was critical to getting the message out. Sean wants the streets to know that he's back, and he's even more cold-hearted than before. You have to find him, Brion, and find him soon. I can help. I got girlfriends all over the city. D.C. is small. Somebody has to know something about him, something

171

that we can use to find him. Sean Branch is from Langdon Park, but he grew up in the Montana section of Northeast. Not sure who his family is and if there's any relatives who still hang out there. He beat the retrial, so I know he's not on parole or anything. Can't catch him at the PO's office. I think he has a kid; I'm not sure. I need to make some calls."

"What about the other dude?" I asked Bionca.

"What other dude?" she replied

"The dude who was with Sean when he killed Crud. The one who killed Whistle."

"Oh, him. What did you say his name was again?"

"Quran. Like the Islamic Holy book."

"Quran, spelled like the book the Muslims believe in? I've heard of him, too. Another vicious killer, from what I hear. His father was a street legend in the city. I know a few bitches that used to talk about him all the time. About his eyes. Said they were gray, I believe. A brown-skinned nigga with light gray eyes. He's about my age, I think. He's from Southeast somewhere." Bionca began to pace the floor again. "Over by Sheridan Terrace, Barry Farms, Wellington Park…somewhere in that area. I know that because my girl Shawnie used to live around there. She knew him from the neighborhood. Talked about him and his brothers all the fuckin' time. Can't remember the brothers' names. But I remember Quran's. Give me a few days and let me see what I can find out about Sean Branch and Mr. Gray-eyed Quran. I'll call you when I know something."

"A'ight, sis. I'm out. I love you."

"Love you too, Brion. Love you too."

Chapter 24
GREG GAMBLE
U.S. District Court
Washington, D.C.
9 a.m.

"Danielle John and Joanna Perales on the behalf of the defendant, Antone White, Your Honor. Mr. White is not present."

"And for the government?" Judge Howard Benson asked.

"United States Attorney Greg Gamble on behalf of the government, Your Honor."

"Well, I must say that this matter before us today must be a very important matter in order for you to make an appearance here today, Mr. Gamble."

I smiled my best smile. "This matter is important to me, Your Honor. The 'First Street Crew' was one of the most dangerous crews of men to walk the streets of D.C. in the late eighties and early nineties. I want to ensure that these men never step foot in our communities again."

"Well, on that note, why don't you start off these proceedings, Mr. Gamble."

"Thank you, Your Honor. In 1994, Antone White, Erick Hicks, and Ronald Hughes were sentenced to life in prison after a jury found them guilty of drug trafficking and racketeering conspiracy offenses, stemming from White's and Hicks's leadership of, and Hughes's membership in, The First Street Crew, from early 1988 until the defendants' arrests approximately five years later. This crew sold large quantities of crack cocaine that has had an ominous effect on our communities here in Washington, D.C. until this day. They engaged in violent acts, including murder and witness intimidation. Now, twenty years later, White and Hicks seek reductions in their sentences to time served and Ronald Hughes seeks a reduction in his supervised release term, based on section 404 of the Fair Sentencing Act of 2010. It's necessary, Your Honor, to put in context for the resolution of the motions the defendants have filed, a more in-depth summary of the defendant's offense conduct, convictions, and sentences, largely drawn from the defendant's sentencing hearings and related documents. Let's also include the D.C. circuit's review of the defendant's direct appeals. This crew operated in the area of First and Thomas Streets in Northwest. Antone White orchestrated the group's activities, working with several friends, including Erick Hicks from the outset and Ronald Hughes, who began working with White in 1990. Although White initially sold small amounts of cocaine, he soon became a wholesale supplier. He sold 'weight' and fronted his cohorts small amounts of cocaine to sell for him..."

***

"So, what do you think Judge Benson is gonna do?" Ari Weinstein asked.

We exited the federal court together and walked over to the Superior Court building.

"I think Judge Benson is going to see the facts. And the facts are exactly what I said they were. Antone White should not receive a reduction to his life sentence under the Fair Sentencing Act due to the change in the crack laws. He was convicted of selling in excess of 30 kilograms of crack cocaine. That's 30 thousand grams of crack. Even if you convert that number to fit 100 to 1 ratio and make it retroactive, three hundred grams of crack in conjunction with the murders, witness intimidation, and gun offenses, the sentence stays the same. Life in prison. Judge Howard Benson has been appointed chief Judge in federal court. I think he's smart enough to see that."

"What about Hughes and Hicks? Your argument opposing their sentence reductions wasn't as strong."

"I don't give a damn about Erick Hicks and Ronald Hughes. If they get out of prison, so be it. It's Antone White that I'm most concerned about."

"Buy why, Greg?"

I stopped walking mid-stride, turned, and faced Ari Weinstein. "Because every confidential informant, cooperator, and rat that we

If You Cross Me Once 2

have on our side over the age of thirty-five is deathly afraid of him. He's the boogeyman to them, Ari, and a man who's been in prison twenty years still having that kind of effect on men and women who are working with us, that scares me. Does that answer your question?"

"I guess it does, Greg. I guess it does."

***

Susan Rosenthal, Ann Sloan, and Ari Weinstein barged into my office unannounced.

"Greg, I need to know whether or not we're offering Kenny Hampton a plea once he gets back to D.C.," Ari said.

"Where is Kenny Hampton at this very moment?"

"He's at FMC Lexington having surgery to repair torn muscles in his shoulder. At the conclusion of that surgery, he's being sent back to the city on a writ from the courts. You never told me what your position is with him."

"I sent Kenny Hampton and Tyrone Clipper to prison when?"

"In 1999. Fourteen years ago."

"And his charge was felony murder, correct?"

"Correct. Felony murder and kidnapping."

"He needs to do at least six to nine more years."

"Got it," Ari said and rushed out.

"How can I help you, Ann?" I said and went back to reading a file on Donzell McCauley's compassionate release.

"James Bassil was killed at Hope Village Halfway house yesterday."

"And I should care for what reason, Ann? He helped us convict Raphael Parker and Antoine Achwith already. So remind me why I should care about James Bassil."

"Greg, I understand that you're getting older, but you haven't reached the Alzheimer stage yet. Antoine Achwith and Raphael Parker were recently granted a new trial in front of Judge Franklin Weisburg. And 'Pig' - James Bassil - was going to get on the stand against them. Without him, Achwith and Parker walk."

175

"Ann, instead of standing here complaining to me about a dead witness, go back through the files. That case is almost twenty years old. And see if we can secure another witness against Parker and Achwith."

Ann Sloan's face turned pink, then she turned and walked out.

Susan Rosenthal quietly walked to the office door and closed it. "Are you ready to discuss this Michael Carter / Maryann Settles thing?"

I leaned back in my chair. "I am. I put someone on Maryann Settles and her husband. They live at——"

"3122 Goldstone Village Drive in Brandywine, Maryland," Susan said and smirked.

I leaned forward, a look of surprise on my face.

"Remember what you told me the other night, Greg? Don't look so surprised. I've been fucking Carlos Trinidad for the last ten years, right? I know everything there is to know about Christopher and Maryann Settles that there is to know. What I need to know from you, right here and right now, is how do you want to play this?"

Suddenly, a wicked smile crossed my face. "I knew that I liked you for reasons other than beauty, brains, ass, and titties, even if I'm not into that sort of thing. Let's try talking to them first. You talk to Maryann and I'll take the husband. See how that goes. And I'll go and meet with Jon Zucker, see if he and I can make some sort of deal."

"And if all of that fails, then what?" Susan asked.

"You're the one in bed with a notorious murderer. You tell me?"

For the next thirty minutes, Susan Rosenthal did exactly that. She told me exactly how we had to deal with our problem. And I couldn't agree more.

***

"Greg Gamble. Can't really say that I'm glad to see you," Jonathan Zucker said as he rose to shake my hand.

"Likewise, Jon, but I'm here bearing gifts/ I hope that I can get just a few moments of your time."

"You're here - albeit, unannounced - but you're here. I'm here. Let's talk. What are these gifts that you say you bring?"

Jon Zucker's office was huge. The decor was opulent. The big money was in criminal defense law. He knew it and so did I. "You have a few clients, Jon——"

"I have several clients, Greg."

"Please, let me finish. Kenny Hampton is in the feds, you filed as 23-110 on his behalf. Michael Wonson is also a client of yours. He's back at the D.C. jail on writ for an evidentiary hearing. You're also defending Jamal Johnson on a PCP and felon in possession of a firearm charge."

"You're well informed, I see. But then again, you should be. You are the U.S. Attorney for the District of Columbia," Zucker replied sarcastically.

"I will tell my people not to fight the sentence reductions for Hampton and Wonson, and I'll offer Johnson a cop to two years."

"That's well below the mandatory minimum of five years."

"I'm aware of that, Jon."

"And you'd do all of the above for what reason, Greg? What am I missing?"

"You're not missing anything. I'm simply requesting a little quid pro quo."

"Quid pro quo?"

"Yeah, actually a three for one."

"Just cut to the chase, Greg, and tell me exactly what it is that you want from me," Jon Zucker said and leaned forward in his seat.

"I need you to back off on the Michael Carter case, and for that, I'll give you whatever you want on the cases I mentioned."

Jon smiled, then laughed. "You're kidding, right? Are you asking me to give the Carter case to someone else? Is that what you mean by back off? Or are you asking me to sell him out?"

It was my turn to smile. "Your words, not mine, but the latter sounds about right."

"I know that you're super busy over at the Triple Nickel, Greg, but I assumed that you got out of the office enough to know that this ain't 1994 or five or six. Shit like that isn't done anymore."

"I'd beg to differ, Jon, and before you go getting up on your high horse, need I remind you of the Marlon White, also known as Cochise Shakur, case? You were his lawyer on that case."

"Are you trying to blackmail me, Mr. Gamble?"

"Blackmail is a strong word with negative connotations. I'd rather say I'm just reminding you of a few things. Like the deals you made on the Kevin Grey case when you represented John Rayner. And the one you made to sell out Maurice 'Poo Poo' Proctor on that K Street conspiracy. Bernard Johnson, Patrick Andrews, Jayvan Allen…need I say more?"

Jon Zucker smiled again. "Zin Carter was right. She said that you were going to fight her father's release. Why now, Greg? Out of all the times you could've walked through that door, sat down in that chair, and offered me deals on hundreds of people, why now? Why this case? And something just dawned on me. I haven't filed any motions in this case. None. So how do you even know about Michael Carter even having a case?"

"Jon, you should know the answer to that. Behind my back, people call me the Wizard of Oz. So, like the great Wizard, I know everything. And to answer your question about why this case, why I chose this case to visit you, there are skeletons in the closet that I'd prefer to keep there. If this case gets the light of day, these skeletons will be revealed, and that would be bad for a lot of people. Listen, you don't have to make a decision right now. Give it a few days, think about what I said. I'm open to switching up the people I offered you deals on. Make a list and give it to me. Either way, I'll be in touch by the middle of next week. I hope that you and I can possibly help each other. In the event that we can't, I'm gonna be very upset that you turned me down, Jon. And I don't think you're going to like me when I'm upset."

"Is that a threat, Greg?" Jon Zucker asked, his face screwed up.

"No threats, Jon. Just promises. And I promise you that you'll go down if I do. These skeletons that I just referenced, they have relatives that live in our closets, too. If mine gets exposed, so does yours. Remember that."

"Get the fuck out of my office!"

Smiling, I rose from my seat, looked around at Jon Zucker's office again. "This office is really nice, Jon, Imagine losing it." I turned and walked out.

Anthony Fields

Chapter 25
MIKE CARTER
USP CANAAN
Waymart, Pennsylvania

"Let's go, Carter." The CO said at the cell door. "You got a legal call scheduled with the counselor." He popped the food slot. "You ready?"

I slipped on my Timberland boots and tied them both up. I walked to the cell door and turned around to cuff. "I'm ready."

"Stick your hands out the wicket."

I complied with the CO's demands. My wrists were cuffed behind my back.

"When I open the door, back out for me, Carter. We're still on lockdown."

I kept facing the back of the cell. Once the door opened, I backed out my cell and was led to the back of the unit where the counselor's office was.

"Fournette," the CO announced. "Here's Carter for his legal call."

"A'ight," counselor John Fournette answered. "Sit down, Carter."

I sat in the chair opposite the counselor's desk. He dialed a number on his landline phone.

"The law office of Jonathan Zucker," a female voice said.

"My name is counselor Fournette at United States Penitentiary Canaan. Inmate Michael Carter has a legal call scheduled for ten a.m. with Attorney Zucker."

"Okay, sir. Can you please hold."

"I'll hold."

A few minutes later, Jonathan Zucker came on the line. "Hello, this is Jonathan Zucker. Mike, is that you?"

"I'm here," I called out.

"Carter, get up so that I can pull your chair up closer. Then I'm going to leave the room for a while and let you talk to your lawyer unmonitored."

I waited until the counselor had left before speaking again. "Jon, what's up? What's the word?"

"Hey, Mike. How are you holding up in there under the circumstances?" Jon Zucker asked.

"I'm as good as can be. We still on lockdown up here, but it's cool. I'm used to it. What's the word on that affidavit situation?"

"I don't know what you did to piss off Greg Gamble, but everything that Zin said was on point."

"And what did Zin say?"

"She said that, uh, that Greg Gamble was going to call in favors and work his political connections to keep you in prison. She said that we're in for the fight of our lives because he's not going to go away or lie down and roll over. And goddangit, she was right."

"Why do you say that?"

"Because that sonofabitch came to my office yesterday. He tried the peaceful, let's make a deal approach first. He wanted to get me to agree to railroad your case in exchange for good outcomes on three of my other clients' cases."

"What?" I exclaimed.

"You heard me right. He called it quid pro quo. If I agreed to sell you out, he'd agree to let three of my clients go home. Three of them."

"Wait a minute . Did you file any of the motions yet?"

"Nope. Not one. I've been going over them to make sure everything is in order. I wanna make sure that my arguments are airtight before I do file them."

"So, if you didn't file anything, how does Gamble even know what we're about to do?"

"Your guess is as good as mine, Mike. I wondered the same thing. Even asked Gamble how he knew about our situation being as though we haven't filed anything."

"What did he say?!"

"Fed me some bullshit about him knowing everything and all this and that. That's bullshit, of course, but it's definitely concerning. The only people I've talked to about this case is you, Zin, and Maryann Settles. That's four of us, and I knew that you, me, and

If You Cross Me Once 2

Zin didn't tell him. Don't see what benefit Maryann Settles would have by contacting Greg Gamble. If it wasn't her——"

Jon Zucker stopped talking mid-sentence. There was a long pause on his ed of the phone.

"Jon, you still there?" I asked.

"I'm here, Mike. A thought just crossed my mind. I can't prove it, but I think Gary Kelman read the affidavit and for some reason, he gave Gamble a heads up about it. I'm thinking that maybe Gamble has something on Gary and Gary paid his debt by telling Gamble about the affidavit. That's what I think, anyway. And it makes sense.

"So, what's the next move? You selling me out or playing the game fair?"

"Let me tell you something. Years ago, I did a lot of shit that I ain't proud of. Made a lot of bad deals - shady side deals. I'm not gonna sit here and act like my thirty years practicing law in D.C. has been angelic, because it hasn't. I made a lot of mistakes that I wish I could take back. I know that, and Greg Gamble knows it. After the peace routine and the quid pro quo thing he threw out there, next came the threats - threats to expose my past shiesty dealings. I'm fifty-four years old and I'm filthy fucking rich. I can retire tomorrow and never worry about a thing ever again. Especially not money. I've invested well, and I own a whole lot of shit. Stocks, bonds, real estate, small businesses, crypto currency. I'm one smart Jew muthafucka, Mike. I always knew how to play the long game. Threatening me was a mistake on Greg Gamble's part. Not only am I not going to sell you out; I'm gonna get you out of prison at no extra cost to you. That will be my final 'screw you' to Gamble and all of his schmuck cronies at the Triple Nickel. Greg Gamble is a fucking fairy and thinks nobody knows it. If he wants to fuck with me, he can be my guest. This old guy has a lot of gas left in the tank, so he can take his feelings and threats and shove them up his ass where all the dicks be. The Jews toppled Jesus, they say. Just wait and see what I do to Greg Gamble. You trust me, Mike?"

"I trust you, Jon. Just get me out of here. That's how we screw Greg Gamble."

183

"I got you, kiddo. I'm going to file some shit today. Can't wait to see Gamble's face after that. He'll have my answer then. A big, fat, 'fuck you'. After I file all of the stuff I've been working on, I'll mail you copies of everything. Sound good to you?"

"Sounds good to me. And thanks, Jon, for everything."

"Don't mention it, Mike. You take care of yourself in there."

"I will, Jon. Be safe. I'm out."

***

"What is the lawyer talkin' 'bout, Mike? Some good shit?" Lil Man asked as soon as I was back in the cell.

"Yeah, homie," I replied. "All good shit. Says he's gonna get me home."

"That's what's up, slim. I'm waiting on that IRAA law to pass. That 18 to 24 joint that the city council in D.C. voting on. They pass that joint, and I'ma be out there with you."

"That would be a good look, homie. Real live."

"Yeah. You can get home and do all the shit you been telling me about. Did you ever let your youngboy——"

"Who, Quran?"

"Yeah. Did you ever tell him that you know he's messing with your daughter?"

"Naw. Never said a word about it."

"Why is that, slim?"

"Because it ain't time yet. Everything has its time. And it ain't his time to know yet. But he will soon, homie. He will soon. Everybody else is playing checkers. I'm playing chess. All things will be revealed in time."

Chapter 26
DAVID BATTLE
D.C. Jail

Every housing unit had two sides to it, the left and the right side, a top and a bottom tier, twenty cells on each tier. The fiberglass encased CO station was called the Bubble. Inside the Bubble were two female correctional officers. Out on the floor was one African male CO named Obula.

I walked past the Bubble after leaving my cell. The unit had twelve phones mounted to the wall, six on the left side and six on the right side. The first phone on the wall was one that I always used when I was outside of the cell. I tapped the dude using the phone and said, "Who's next on the phone?"

"You are," the dude replied and went back to his call.

Ten minutes later, the call was finished and the dude left the phone receiver dangling. I picked up the receiver as I sat on the bench connected to the table that lined the common area. I dialed a couple numbers, but couldn't get through. I decided to call Jihad since I couldn't reach Quran.

Jihad answered the call on the second ring. After the recording played through, he pressed one and said, "What's up, slim?"

"Ain't shit. What's up with bruh? Why he ain't answering his phone?"

"Because he got a new one. We all got new ones. I was supposed to trash this one, but I haven't done it yet. I'ma get at you with the new numbers soon."

"That's what's up. Everybody good?"

"Good as can be. How are you? What's the word on the situation?"

"That's what I wanted bruh to know. They dismissed the body this morning. Didn't even have to go to court. Now, I'm just fighting the gun charge. My lawyer's trying to get me a cop to time served, but the prosecutor nigga is playing hard ball. They mad because I beat the body. I talk——" I turned my head and looked up to see a dude with his dick out, stroking it while beaming in on the two female COs in the Bubble. My blood boiled and my anger rose. "Let me hit you back, Jay. I gotta go," I said and replaced the receiver onto the hook.

The dude who was hitting the female COs in the Bubble was oblivious to everyone around him. His perverted mind enveloped his being and made him reckless. In prison, what the young dude was doing had a name: gunning or jacking. Hitting heads was the term that was used by everyone outside the game. It was super disrespectful for any man to pull out his dick in a space full of other men. I moved with alacrity to my cell. I moved with emotion and purpose.

It only took me a minute to get my flip-out street knife out of my spot in the cell. I slid out the cell and walked up the tier and then the steps that led to the top tier, to my target. The creep was still at it, oblivious to the animal that was coming his way. By the time he realized that death was near, it was too late. My first shot with the knife hit him high in the shoulder.

"A-a-a-r-r-g-g-h!" the dude cried out. "What——"

I was in beast mode, totally impervious to the dude's cries. I stabbed him again. He took off running down the tier. I followed in hot pursuit.

"What I do? What did I do?"

The doomed man ran to the end of the tier and couldn't navigate the sharp turn that would have put him on the other side of the tier. He ran into the wall and fell to the ground. I stood over the fallen man. I swaddled his outstretched arms that flailed and picked my shots. My knife slammed into the creep from all different angles.

"Please…a-a-r-r-g-g-h…don't…kill…me!"

"Shut up, bitch! You like to play with your dick in public, right.? Take what comes with it!" I replied as I blacked out.

The next thing I knew, I was tackled from the back. The knife was pried from my hand.

***

If You Cross Me Once 2

In the holding cage in medical, I laid on the metal bench and must have fallen asleep. But then I was awakened by the call of my name. I opened my eyes and sat up. The man standing on the other side of the bars a familiar face to me. It was none other than Greg Gamble.

"David, David, David." Greg Gamble smiled. "I knew that you'd do something to fuck up your release from jail. All you had to do was chill out and eventually you would have walked out of this place. But you couldn't chill, could you? All the men in this jail today understand is violence, right?

And you definitely speak the language of jail. That kid had the audacity to be beating his meat out on the tier. Disrespected you, right? And you made him pay for it just like you did Solomon "Manny" Robinson.

I couldn't get you on the Robinson murder, David, but I got you on this one. That kid you stabbed . . . . Warren Stevenson. Well, he died about an hour ago at UMC . . . . and guess what? I'm dropping the gun case just to prosecute you on this new murder. But guess what else, David? I can help you. I can make the new murder charge go away. All you have to do is confess your sins. Confess to the Robinson murder and tell me who killed Yolanda Stevens, Thomas Caldwell and Khitab Bashir.

I know that Quran Bashir was responsible for those murders, but I need you to say that. Give me Quran Bashir and I promise you, you get to go home. What's it gonna be, David"

To Be Continued…
If You Cross Me 3
Coming Soon

Anthony Fields

NOTE FROM THE AUTHOR

It's sad that I have to say this after every book I write, but none of the events written in this book are real. None of this stuff actually happened. Everything inside this book is the imagination of the author gone wild. I push myself to come off as realistic as possible, although the scenes and scenarios are real. David Battle is a childhood friend who's been out of prison for eleven years and has never gone back. He's married to a wonderful woman named Tawana and he works for Catholic Charities. He's inspiring other ex-convicts and empowering the youth with his work. Sean Branch is also a real person, but none of the violence I have attributed to him is real. None of it. But I will say that several of the people killed in this book are real people, yet they remain alive. They have all dishonored themselves and violated the code, yet they still live. I won't say who they are here, but they know who they are.

And speaking of violating the code of silence, I have a platform to speak and get my words out to the masses. I was recently confronted with the slander and lies that have been following me. I was told that a guy had my name in his mouth, repeating the lies spawned by a coward. I went into full Jason mode. When I stepped to the guy who was alleged to have mouthed the slander, he swore on everything in the heavens and earth that he'd never said anything about me. After I calmed down, I realized that I was about to throw my life away to defend my honor. All the good men around me begged me to not do that.

"You're chasing ghosts," they say. "No one is ever going to stand on what they say out of your presence."

I agree with all of that, but still I stand determined to die about my name, my honor, my legacy. The 48 laws of power say that when you build a certain reputation, you have to protect it. I agree with that, and I will do that until they cover my face with dirt.

A good man once told me that the lion doesn't always have to roar to prove he's the king of the jungle. Well, in my case, I do. I pray that everyone who reads this can hear me roar. I never got weak. Never proffered. Never debriefed. Never interviewed. Never implicated anyone at trial. Never told on anyone. Never. I swear that three times, by Allah. I was in Alexandria Detention center when last at trial. My codefendant, Lenell "L" Tucker was at D.C. jail. He ran around the jail and told anyone who'd listen that I told on the case. I wasn't there to defend against his lies. And now, he's at Petersburg Medium in Virginia and won't even stand on the lies he started.

People love to condemn authors for the stories they put in their books. So I say again to whom it may concern, this entire book is based on fiction. It's completely made up. None of it is real.

Before I go, I gotta shout out Antone White and Eric Hicks, who've finally made it home after almost thirty years in prison.

DC, stand up!
Buckeyfields

Anthony Fields

Lock Down Publications and Ca$h Presents assisted publishing packages.

BASIC PACKAGE $499
Editing
Cover Design
Formatting

UPGRADED PACKAGE $800
Typing
Editing
Cover Design
Formatting

ADVANCE PACKAGE $1,200
Typing
Editing
Cover Design
Formatting
Copyright registration
Proofreading
Upload book to Amazon

LDP SUPREME PACKAGE $1,500
Typing
Editing
Cover Design
Formatting
Copyright registration
Proofreading
Set up Amazon account
Upload book to Amazon
Advertise on LDP Amazon and Facebook page

***Other services available upon request. Additional charges may apply

Lock Down Publications
P.O. Box 944
Stockbridge, GA 30281-9998
Phone # 470 303-9761

Anthony Fields

Submission Guideline

Submit the first three chapters of your completed manuscript to ldpsubmissions@gmail.com, subject line: Your book's title. The manuscript must be in a .doc file and sent as an attachment. Document should be in Times New Roman, double spaced and in size 12 font. Also, provide your synopsis and full contact information. If sending multiple submissions, they must each be in a separate email.

Have a story but no way to send it electronically? You can still submit to LDP/Ca$h Presents. Send in the first three chapters, written or typed, of your completed manuscript to:

LDP: Submissions Dept
Po Box 944
Stockbridge, Ga 30281

DO NOT send original manuscript. Must be a duplicate.

Provide your synopsis and a cover letter containing your full contact information.

Thanks for considering LDP and Ca$h Presents.

If You Cross Me Once 2

NEW RELEASES

THE BRICK MAN 5 by KING RIO
BABY I'M WINTERTIME COLD 2 by MEESHA
MONEY MAFIA 2 by JIBRIL WILLIAMS
REAL G'S MOVE IN SILENCE by VON DIESEL
IF YOU CROSS ME ONCE 2 by ANTHONY FIELDS

Anthony Fields

<u>Coming Soon from Lock Down Publications/Ca$h Presents</u>

BLOOD OF A BOSS **VI**

SHADOWS OF THE GAME II

TRAP BASTARD II

By **Askari**

LOYAL TO THE GAME **IV**

By **T.J. & Jelissa**

TRUE SAVAGE **VIII**

MIDNIGHT CARTEL IV

DOPE BOY MAGIC IV

CITY OF KINGZ III

NIGHTMARE ON SILENT AVE II

THE PLUG OF LIL MEXICO II

CLASSIC CITY II

By **Chris Green**

BLAST FOR ME **III**

A SAVAGE DOPEBOY III

CUTTHROAT MAFIA III

DUFFLE BAG CARTEL VII

HEARTLESS GOON VI

By **Ghost**

A HUSTLER'S DECEIT III

KILL ZONE II

BAE BELONGS TO ME III

TIL DEATH II

By **Aryanna**

KING OF THE TRAP III

By **T.J. Edwards**

GORILLAZ IN THE BAY V

3X KRAZY III

If You Cross Me Once 2

STRAIGHT BEAST MODE III
De'Kari
KINGPIN KILLAZ IV
STREET KINGS III
PAID IN BLOOD III
CARTEL KILLAZ IV
DOPE GODS III
Hood Rich
SINS OF A HUSTLA II
ASAD
YAYO V
Bred In The Game 2
S. Allen
THE STREETS WILL TALK II
By Yolanda Moore
SON OF A DOPE FIEND III
HEAVEN GOT A GHETTO II
SKI MASK MONEY II
By Renta
LOYALTY AIN'T PROMISED III
By Keith Williams
I'M NOTHING WITHOUT HIS LOVE II
SINS OF A THUG II
TO THE THUG I LOVED BEFORE II
IN A HUSTLER I TRUST II
By Monet Dragun
QUIET MONEY IV
EXTENDED CLIP III
THUG LIFE IV
By **Trai'Quan**

Anthony Fields

THE STREETS MADE ME IV
By **Larry D. Wright**
IF YOU CROSS ME ONCE III
ANGEL V
By **Anthony Fields**
THE STREETS WILL NEVER CLOSE IV
By K'ajji
HARD AND RUTHLESS III
KILLA KOUNTY IV
By Khufu
MONEY GAME III
By Smoove Dolla
JACK BOYS VS DOPE BOYS IV
A GANGSTA'S QUR'AN V
COKE GIRLZ II
COKE BOYS II
LIFE OF A SAVAGE V
CHI'RAQ GANGSTAS V
By Romell Tukes
MURDA WAS THE CASE III
Elijah R. Freeman
THE STREETS NEVER LET GO III
By Robert Baptiste
AN UNFORESEEN LOVE IV
BABY, I'M WINTERTIME COLD III
By **Meesha**

QUEEN OF THE ZOO III
By **Black Migo**
VICIOUS LOYALTY III

If You Cross Me Once 2

By Kingpen
A GANGSTA'S PAIN III
By J-Blunt
CONFESSIONS OF A JACKBOY III
By Nicholas Lock
GRIMEY WAYS III
By Ray Vinci
KING KILLA II
By Vincent "Vitto" Holloway
BETRAYAL OF A THUG III
By Fre$h
THE MURDER QUEENS III
By Michael Gallon
THE BIRTH OF A GANGSTER III
By Delmont Player
TREAL LOVE II
By Le'Monica Jackson
FOR THE LOVE OF BLOOD III
By Jamel Mitchell
RAN OFF ON DA PLUG II
By Paper Boi Rari
HOOD CONSIGLIERE III
By Keese
PRETTY GIRLS DO NASTY THINGS II
By Nicole Goosby
PROTÉGÉ OF A LEGEND II
By Corey Robinson
IT'S JUST ME AND YOU II
By Ah'Million
BORN IN THE GRAVE III

Anthony Fields

By Self Made Tay
FOREVER GANGSTA III
By Adrian Dulan
GORILLAZ IN THE TRENCHES II
By SayNoMore
THE COCAINE PRINCESS VI
By King Rio
CRIME BOSS II
Playa Ray
LOYALTY IS EVERYTHING II
Molotti
HERE TODAY GONE TOMORROW II
By Fly Rock
REAL G'S MOVE IN SILENCE II
By Von Diesel

Available Now

RESTRAINING ORDER **I & II**
By **CA$H & Coffee**
LOVE KNOWS NO BOUNDARIES **I II & III**
By **Coffee**
RAISED AS A GOON I, II, III & IV
BRED BY THE SLUMS I, II, III
BLAST FOR ME I & II
ROTTEN TO THE CORE I II III
A BRONX TALE I, II, III
DUFFLE BAG CARTEL I II III IV V VI

If You Cross Me Once 2

HEARTLESS GOON I II III IV V
A SAVAGE DOPEBOY I II
DRUG LORDS I II III
CUTTHROAT MAFIA I II
KING OF THE TRENCHES
By **Ghost**
LAY IT DOWN **I & II**
LAST OF A DYING BREED I II
BLOOD STAINS OF A SHOTTA I & II III
By **Jamaica**
LOYAL TO THE GAME I II III
LIFE OF SIN I, II III
By **TJ & Jelissa**
BLOODY COMMAS I & II
SKI MASK CARTEL I II & III
KING OF NEW YORK I II,III IV V
RISE TO POWER I II III
COKE KINGS I II III IV V
BORN HEARTLESS I II III IV
KING OF THE TRAP I II
By **T.J. Edwards**
IF LOVING HIM IS WRONG…I & II
LOVE ME EVEN WHEN IT HURTS I II III
By **Jelissa**
WHEN THE STREETS CLAP BACK I & II III
THE HEART OF A SAVAGE I II III IV
MONEY MAFIA I II
LOYAL TO THE SOIL I II III
By **Jibril Williams**
A DISTINGUISHED THUG STOLE MY HEART I II & III

Anthony Fields

LOVE SHOULDN'T HURT I II III IV
RENEGADE BOYS I II III IV
PAID IN KARMA I II III
SAVAGE STORMS I II III
AN UNFORESEEN LOVE I II III
BABY, I'M WINTERTIME COLD I II

By **Meesha**

A GANGSTER'S CODE I &, II III
A GANGSTER'S SYN I II III
THE SAVAGE LIFE I II III
CHAINED TO THE STREETS I II III
BLOOD ON THE MONEY I II III
A GANGSTA'S PAIN I II

By J-Blunt

PUSH IT TO THE LIMIT

By **Bre' Hayes**

BLOOD OF A BOSS **I, II, III, IV, V**
SHADOWS OF THE GAME
TRAP BASTARD

By **Askari**

THE STREETS BLEED MURDER **I, II & III**
THE HEART OF A GANGSTA I II& III

By **Jerry Jackson**

CUM FOR ME I II III IV V VI VII VIII

An **LDP Erotica Collaboration**

BRIDE OF A HUSTLA **I II & II**
THE FETTI GIRLS **I, II& III**
CORRUPTED BY A GANGSTA I, II III, IV
BLINDED BY HIS LOVE
THE PRICE YOU PAY FOR LOVE I, II ,III

If You Cross Me Once 2

DOPE GIRL MAGIC I II III
By **Destiny Skai**
WHEN A GOOD GIRL GOES BAD
By **Adrienne**
THE COST OF LOYALTY I II III
By Kweli
A GANGSTER'S REVENGE **I II III & IV**
THE BOSS MAN'S DAUGHTERS I II III IV V
A SAVAGE LOVE **I & II**
BAE BELONGS TO ME I II
A HUSTLER'S DECEIT I, II, III
WHAT BAD BITCHES DO I, II, III
SOUL OF A MONSTER I II III
KILL ZONE
A DOPE BOY'S QUEEN I II III
TIL DEATH
By **Aryanna**
A KINGPIN'S AMBITON
A KINGPIN'S AMBITION **II**
I MURDER FOR THE DOUGH
By **Ambitious**
TRUE SAVAGE I II III IV V VI VII
DOPE BOY MAGIC I, II, III
MIDNIGHT CARTEL I II III
CITY OF KINGZ I II
NIGHTMARE ON SILENT AVE
THE PLUG OF LIL MEXICO II
CLASSIC CITY
By **Chris Green**
A DOPEBOY'S PRAYER

Anthony Fields

By **Eddie "Wolf" Lee**
THE KING CARTEL **I, II & III**

By **Frank Gresham**
THESE NIGGAS AIN'T LOYAL **I, II & III**

By **Nikki Tee**
GANGSTA SHYT **I II &III**

By **CATO**
THE ULTIMATE BETRAYAL

By **Phoenix**
BOSS'N UP **I , II & III**

By **Royal Nicole**
I LOVE YOU TO DEATH

By **Destiny J**
I RIDE FOR MY HITTA
I STILL RIDE FOR MY HITTA

By **Misty Holt**
LOVE & CHASIN' PAPER

By **Qay Crockett**
TO DIE IN VAIN
SINS OF A HUSTLA

By **ASAD**
BROOKLYN HUSTLAZ

By **Boogsy Morina**
BROOKLYN ON LOCK I & II

By **Sonovia**
GANGSTA CITY

By **Teddy Duke**
A DRUG KING AND HIS DIAMOND I & II III
A DOPEMAN'S RICHES
HER MAN, MINE'S TOO I, II

If You Cross Me Once 2

CASH MONEY HO'S
THE WIFEY I USED TO BE I II
PRETTY GIRLS DO NASTY THINGS
By Nicole Goosby
TRAPHOUSE KING **I II & III**
KINGPIN KILLAZ I II III
STREET KINGS I II
PAID IN BLOOD **I II**
CARTEL KILLAZ I II III
DOPE GODS I II
By **Hood Rich**
LIPSTICK KILLAH **I, II, III**
CRIME OF PASSION I II & III
FRIEND OR FOE I II III
By **Mimi**
STEADY MOBBN' **I, II, III**
THE STREETS STAINED MY SOUL I II III
By **Marcellus Allen**
WHO SHOT YA **I, II, III**
SON OF A DOPE FIEND I II
HEAVEN GOT A GHETTO
SKI MASK MONEY
Renta
GORILLAZ IN THE BAY **I II III IV**
TEARS OF A GANGSTA I II
3X KRAZY I II
STRAIGHT BEAST MODE I II
DE'KARI
TRIGGADALE I II III
MURDAROBER WAS THE CASE I II

Anthony Fields

Elijah R. Freeman
GOD BLESS THE TRAPPERS I, II, III
THESE SCANDALOUS STREETS I, II, III
FEAR MY GANGSTA I, II, III IV, V
THESE STREETS DON'T LOVE NOBODY I, II
BURY ME A G I, II, III, IV, V
A GANGSTA'S EMPIRE I, II, III, IV
THE DOPEMAN'S BODYGAURD I II
THE REALEST KILLAZ I II III
THE LAST OF THE OGS I II III

Tranay Adams
THE STREETS ARE CALLING

Duquie Wilson
MARRIED TO A BOSS I II III

By Destiny Skai & Chris Green
KINGZ OF THE GAME I II III IV V VI
CRIME BOSS

Playa Ray
SLAUGHTER GANG I II III
RUTHLESS HEART I II III

By Willie Slaughter
FUK SHYT

By Blakk Diamond
DON'T F#CK WITH MY HEART I II

By Linnea
ADDICTED TO THE DRAMA I II III
IN THE ARM OF HIS BOSS II

By Jamila
YAYO I II III IV
A SHOOTER'S AMBITION I II

If You Cross Me Once 2

BRED IN THE GAME
By S. Allen
TRAP GOD I II III
RICH $AVAGE I II III
MONEY IN THE GRAVE I II III
By Martell Troublesome Bolden
FOREVER GANGSTA I II
GLOCKS ON SATIN SHEETS I II
By Adrian Dulan
TOE TAGZ I II III IV
LEVELS TO THIS SHYT I II
IT'S JUST ME AND YOU
By Ah'Million
KINGPIN DREAMS I II III
RAN OFF ON DA PLUG
By Paper Boi Rari
CONFESSIONS OF A GANGSTA I II III IV
CONFESSIONS OF A JACKBOY I II
By Nicholas Lock
I'M NOTHING WITHOUT HIS LOVE
SINS OF A THUG
TO THE THUG I LOVED BEFORE
A GANGSTA SAVED XMAS
IN A HUSTLER I TRUST
By Monet Dragun
CAUGHT UP IN THE LIFE I II III
THE STREETS NEVER LET GO I II
By Robert Baptiste
NEW TO THE GAME I II III
MONEY, MURDER & MEMORIES I II III

Anthony Fields

By **Malik D. Rice**
LIFE OF A SAVAGE I II III IV
A GANGSTA'S QUR'AN I II III IV
MURDA SEASON I II III
GANGLAND CARTEL I II III
CHI'RAQ GANGSTAS I II III IV
KILLERS ON ELM STREET I II III
JACK BOYZ N DA BRONX I II III
A DOPEBOY'S DREAM I II III
JACK BOYS VS DOPE BOYS I II III
COKE GIRLZ
COKE BOYS
By **Romell Tukes**
LOYALTY AIN'T PROMISED I II
By **Keith Williams**
QUIET MONEY I II III
THUG LIFE I II III
EXTENDED CLIP I II
A GANGSTA'S PARADISE
By **Trai'Quan**
THE STREETS MADE ME I II III
By **Larry D. Wright**
THE ULTIMATE SACRIFICE I, II, III, IV, V, VI
KHADIFI
IF YOU CROSS ME ONCE I II
ANGEL I II III IV
IN THE BLINK OF AN EYE
By **Anthony Fields**
THE LIFE OF A HOOD STAR
By **Ca$h & Rashia Wilson**

If You Cross Me Once 2

THE STREETS WILL NEVER CLOSE I II III
By K'ajji
CREAM I II III
THE STREETS WILL TALK
By Yolanda Moore
NIGHTMARES OF A HUSTLA I II III
By King Dream
CONCRETE KILLA I II III
VICIOUS LOYALTY I II
By Kingpen
HARD AND RUTHLESS I II
MOB TOWN 251
THE BILLIONAIRE BENTLEYS I II III
REAL G'S MOVE IN SILENCE
By Von Diesel
GHOST MOB
Stilloan Robinson
MOB TIES I II III IV V VI
SOUL OF A HUSTLER, HEART OF A KILLER
GORILLAZ IN THE TRENCHES
By SayNoMore
BODYMORE MURDERLAND I II III
THE BIRTH OF A GANGSTER I II
By Delmont Player
FOR THE LOVE OF A BOSS
By C. D. Blue
MOBBED UP I II III IV
THE BRICK MAN I II III IV V
THE COCAINE PRINCESS I II III IV V
By King Rio

Anthony Fields

KILLA KOUNTY I II III IV
By Khufu
MONEY GAME I II
By Smoove Dolla
A GANGSTA'S KARMA I II III
By FLAME
KING OF THE TRENCHES I II III
by **GHOST & TRANAY ADAMS**
QUEEN OF THE ZOO I II
By **Black Migo**
GRIMEY WAYS I II
By Ray Vinci
XMAS WITH AN ATL SHOOTER
By Ca$h & Destiny Skai
KING KILLA
By Vincent "Vitto" Holloway
BETRAYAL OF A THUG I II
By Fre$h
THE MURDER QUEENS I II
By Michael Gallon
TREAL LOVE
By Le'Monica Jackson
FOR THE LOVE OF BLOOD I II
By Jamel Mitchell
HOOD CONSIGLIERE I II
By Keese
PROTÉGÉ OF A LEGEND
By Corey Robinson
BORN IN THE GRAVE I II
By Self Made Tay

If You Cross Me Once 2

MOAN IN MY MOUTH
By XTASY
TORN BETWEEN A GANGSTER AND A GENTLEMAN
By J-BLUNT & Miss Kim
LOYALTY IS EVERYTHING
Molotti
HERE TODAY GONE TOMORROW
By Fly Rock

Anthony Fields

BOOKS BY LDP'S CEO, CA$H

TRUST IN NO MAN
TRUST IN NO MAN 2
TRUST IN NO MAN 3
BONDED BY BLOOD
SHORTY GOT A THUG
THUGS CRY
THUGS CRY 2
THUGS CRY 3
TRUST NO BITCH
TRUST NO BITCH 2
TRUST NO BITCH 3
TIL MY CASKET DROPS
RESTRAINING ORDER
RESTRAINING ORDER 2
IN LOVE WITH A CONVICT
LIFE OF A HOOD STAR
XMAS WITH AN ATL SHOOTER

If You Cross Me Once 2